Dorothy —
you like to read
a lot — my the voo-
woo be with you —

A LESSON
IN WOO-WOO
AND MURDER

DAVID UNGER, PHD

Artwork by Damonza

ISBN: 978-1-7323395-6-9

ALessoninWooWooandMurder.com

Author Note

One of the challenges I faced writing about the 80s is that many of the things we now hold as fundamental values were not in place at the time. I have endeavored to have my characters hold respect for others in the forefront of their interactions, but wanted to stay true to the tenor of the times. Their actions and words might not always be as sensitive as they could be, but historic wrongs can only be righted if we acknowledge them. Where they appear here, they are a deliberately mindful reminder of how far we've come ... and how far we still have to go.

THE LESSON SERIES

A Lesson in Sex and Murder
A Lesson in Music and Murder
A Lesson in Therapy and Murder
A Lesson in Mystery and Murder
A Lesson in Baseball and Murder
A Lesson in Cowboys and Murder
A Lesson in Comedy and Murder
A Lesson in Reunions and Murder
A Lesson in Woo-Woo and Murder
Coming soon
A Lesson in Dogs and Murder
A Lesson in Learning and Murder

THE RELATIONSHIP TRAINING MANUALS

The Relationship Training Manual for Men
The Relationship Training Manual for Men* Women's Edition
Parenting Your Teen: A Relationship Training Manual

It's no wonder that truth is stranger than fiction.
Fiction has to make sense.

Mark Twain

CHAPTER ONE

What the Woo?

Thursday, August 1, 1985

YOU MAY HAVE noticed that there's a certain repetitiveness to my books. My work and life are probably similar to yours in that there's a lot of repetition. I like that. It's comforting. By and large, I know what to expect of the day, and that familiarity is reassuring and provides peace of mind.

I eat the same foods. Visit the same places. Hang out with the same friends. Read the same kinds of books. Watch the same kinds of movies. Go to the same kinds of concerts and events.

Unless I'm being paid.

That's when, while I try to maintain a healthy degree of stability, I have to deal with unknown elements that influence my path.

In 1983, I went to the US Festival and wrote about it in *A Lesson in Music and Murder*. If you haven't read it, this is a small spoiler alert but not a critical one: I met Eve and Sheridan there. They were camped out in a Cherokee tepee. I never found out what Eve did, but Sheridan was a drug dealer and poet.

They'd called me up a couple of weeks ago and made an appointment to see me in my office.

After hugs and perfunctory niceties, Sheridan got to it. "Dave, we need you to help us out. We wouldn't ask you if we didn't believe you had the requisite skills and panache to do the job."

"That's kind of you. Not sure what skills and panache you're wanting, but I'm open to doing what I can to help."

"Yes, Dave, we suspected you'd say that and we want you to say that, but first Eve needs to tell you what we want and then you can decide if you're in or out."

"Okay…"

"I would never ask you to put yourself in harm's way if I didn't think you could navigate your way through," Eve said, and gave me an encouraging smile. "We believe in you. We've seen how you can turn nothing into something."

"Voodoo-therapy magic, Dave," Sheridan said. "You do that. But while we believe in you and your powers, voodoo is only one of many forces at play in the universe."

"Yeah. I get that."

"Dave, we want you listen to what Eve has to say with an open mind."

"I'll see what I can do, although your warm-up is getting my guard up."

"You should be skeptical and wary, Dave, because we're speaking about things you know very little about."

"That covers a lot of ground. Can you be more specific?"

Eve gave me a comforting smile. For a forty-something hippie-esque woman, she did have a certain innocence that made me trust her.

"There are unseen forces in the world. We don't always understand why things happen the way they do. I'm sure you've had moments when something out of the ordinary happens that you can't explain."

"Like when I got my doctorate. My parents still can't figure out how that happened."

"We're having trouble too, Dave, but listen to Eve."

"Researchers, scientists, and neurologists all tell us that we only use a small portion of our brains. Yet there are those among us who've been able to access parts of their brain that others haven't. I meditate and spend time at spiritual retreats and I've come to believe I can feel the forces moving. I don't know how. I don't know what. But I know those forces are coming to the expo. The tide will change."

"Doesn't the tide come in and out on a daily basis?"

"Dave, pay attention. Eve is telling you there's bad juju coming. She can feel the turbulence even if others can't."

"Okay. That's not good. Yet maybe that allows for an ounce of prevention."

"That's why we're here."

"I'm the ounce of prevention?"

"Well, you're not a spoonful of sugar. Nevertheless, Eve believes having you around during the expo will help stem the tide."

"You won't stem it, but at least you can try to end it."

"So wait a minute. You want me to come to the expo and just hang out? And if something untoward happens, put an end to it."

"You're listening, Dave. Yes, that's what we want you to do. That and a few other things."

"Care to elaborate?"

"I don't know what's going to go awry," said Eve. "But something will. I'm sure of it. We have a booth at the expo and we want you with us."

"You want me to stay in the booth for a week?"

"Yes and no. It's Wednesday night through Sunday afternoon. We need you to be around. You don't have to be in the booth the whole time. You just need to make things better. That's what you do, don't you?"

"I try, but as much as I'd like to help you out, I can't just take off that amount of time—not without getting paid."

"Dave, do we look like we were born yesterday? We'll pay you. Not your usual high fee, but you'll value what you get."

"Is there a dollar amount associated with that?"

"Dave, you know relationships are built on trust. You have to trust us with this."

CHAPTER TWO

Out of the Box

Wednesday, August 7, 1985

I'M AN OUT-OF-THE-BOX therapist. I've accompanied clients to a music festival and a baseball camp, and been invited to a cowboy-poetry gathering, a comedy conference, and other out-of-the-office places, all in the line of duty. Usually I quote a price, the client accepts it or we negotiate, and that's that. I was unsure about the take-home pay with Eve and Sheridan, but it was August, the month when most therapists go on vacation because a sizable portion of their clients are on vacation. School was out, I had no classes to teach and only a few clients to reschedule—I was as free as I get. Plus, I was curious.

The Whole Life Expo was a New Age, spiritual, natural health, conscious living, metaphysical, extraterrestrial, enlightening hodge-podge of vendors, speakers, and snake-oil purveyors. Left to my own devices, I'd not have gone.

I had one client who said he might come to Santa Monica to see me at the expo because he might need me. I try to empower my clients so they don't need me. But sometimes they do and, frankly, it makes me feel good when they think I can help them. Often, just thinking I can help them helps them as much as the actual help I provide.

Some of you will remember Bennett. He's been referred to as a high high-maintenance boy- or girlfriend. He wants what he wants when he wants it, and what with his being a *New York Times* best-selling mystery writer, he's used to getting his way. But lately he'd bumped into people who were more used to getting their way. The connected movie producers who'd optioned the rights to Bennett's books made his life richer but constricted.

Bennett hadn't made the best deal with them. There was a morality clause in the small print that Bennett had already broken once when he'd got caught doing coke. Now, he was on a short leash and not liking it because if he got caught again he'd lose his share of the profits. He was wealthy enough to afford blowing his share, but he'd be damned if he'd let the producers get one over on him. He'd also be damned if he'd quit doing coke and fucking hookers.

Would Bennett show up? I wasn't sure. He'd crashed my twentieth high-school reunion a couple of months earlier, and since then had been able to keep his naughty ways under sufficient wraps. He'd told me he was focusing on polishing up the script and that shooting was scheduled to begin soon. He's a dedicated writer so it was possible he was staying on task, yet knowing him the way I do, I wouldn't bet on that lasting long.

CHAPTER THREE

Setting Up

MOST DAYS, THE Santa Monica Civic Auditorium was a thirty-minute drive from my home. For those who live in LA, that's considered a reasonable commute. The event was officially beginning Thursday morning at ten and running through to Sunday at four. There was a private setting-up party Wednesday night for all the vendors and a closing party Sunday.

I had no idea what might be featured in Eve's booth, but I was ready to sign in and see where I'd be headquartered. The Civic had been built back in 1958 and had a bland yet unique architecture. A half-dozen tall pylons supported a cantilevered canopy behind which was a patterned glass wall that supposedly reduced the sun's glare. In its prime, it had been home to the Oscars for six years, and Frank Sinatra, Bob Dylan, David Bowie, Billy Joel, The Village People, Ella Fitzgerald, Bruce Springsteen, the Eagles, and the T.A.M.I. Show with the Rolling Stones and James Brown had all appeared on its stage.

These days the concerts had moved on; smaller trade shows and events had moved in. The place held three thousand for a concert and had enough room for close to a hundred booths. Plus, there was the stage where demonstrations would be taking place.

Eve had told me to register at the entrance and find my way to her booth. I got a lanyard with a name tag and a brochure with a list of all the booths. I went in search of the garden—Eve's Garden.

I made my way down the aisles, taking in the candles, incense, crystals, salves and potions, jewelry vendors, smoothie makers, weight-loss gurus, aural energy readers, mediums, healers, psychic tarot-card readers, chakra balancers, and body workers. I was halfway down the second aisle when I found Eve's Garden.

Eve's Garden had lots of Eve's garden in it. The space was arranged with hanging plants, floor pots full of ficus, and a few good-sized crystals. Eve herself was arranging vials of liquids, small baskets of herbs, and exotic bottles full of their own mysteries on a display table. Two stools at the back would give her and Sheridan a place to get off their feet when they needed a rest. For a small space, she had set it up well.

"Hey there," I said.

"Dave, perfect timing. Eve's gotten me to drag everything in here and help set up. She's putting on the finishing touches. Then we're going to meet our neighbors."

"I'm ready for the tour when you are. If you need it, I'm happy to lend a hand. Especially now that the heavy lifting is over. The booth looks lush and inviting."

"Eve's Garden, Dave. You can't beat that."

"We're glad you're here," Eve said, giving me a welcoming hug. "I have to tell you, I'm awfully excited to be here. I've never done one of these before, and while I have bad vibes about what will happen, there're also positive ones. One thing's for sure—the forces are at play, and whatever happens I'm glad you're here."

"I'm glad to assist. I'm a bit out of my element here, but that's not breaking news."

"Dave," Sheridan said, "do you have an element?"

"I have an ill-defined element."

"Do you believe in realities other than our own?"

"I've learned that my reality isn't always the same as others'. While I tend to take for granted that we're all basically in the same realm, people do stray off."

"We're not talking straying off like you getting lost in your thoughts. We're talking our neighbors over here, Dave. They're the only ones we've met so far and I just know you're going to enjoy meeting them as well."

"If you say so."

"You'll get a kick out of them. They've strayed off a bit more than most. We haven't met the ones on the other side, and we've done nothing more than wave to the ones opposite."

"The aisles aren't that wide so you'll have a little community within the community for yourself."

"That's what you like, Dave. A group. We'll see how neighborly ours is."

CHAPTER FOUR

Where You Been Lately?

You believe in UFOs? You think there's life out there in the universe? Life that's more evolved or less evolved than ours. Maybe both. That's the thing about the unknown; it's unknown. You're welcome to your opinion but the truth has yet to be fully revealed.

Unless, of course, you've been there.

We've all been told not to judge a book by the cover, so I hesitated to judge the UFO booth by its looks. Yet all it had going for it was a couple of guys sitting in lawn chairs under a banner that said: *UFO—Been There, Done That.*

"What's with this booth?" I asked Sheridan.

"You should be careful when you're talking with them. And for heaven's sake, don't touch them."

"Because?"

"First, they'll blow your mind. Second, and I'm not saying I believe them, but they've been to places I only see at night when I gaze up in the sky. Who knows what they picked up? According to the guy I spoke with, they were abducted and spent time with a group of aliens on vacation, visiting various planets and collecting souvenirs."

"The guys were souvenirs?"

"I am. Who's your friend? Wait, let me see if I can conjure up his spirit."

"You're kind of freaking us out," said Sheridan.

"Don't let her spook you," said one of the other women. "She read your name tags."

"Phew. You had me going," I said.

"Don't be fooled," said Madame Vadama. "I may have read your name tag but it doesn't mention that you're a doctor of psychology and a man of mystery."

"You're right, it doesn't. Yet perhaps we're all people of mystery."

"But we're not all doctors of psychology."

"No, we're not. But in many ways we are."

"Yes. That's true."

"So what is the House of Living Dreams?"

"Why don't you come back later and I'll show you? I'm here early every day. They do yoga on the stage. It would be beneficial for you."

Interstellar travelers on one side. Dr. Ketchall and the House of Living Dreams across the aisle. This certainly wasn't Mister Rogers' neighborhood.

CHAPTER SEVEN
Chakra Tuning

I DON'T KNOW if Mister Rogers would have felt any more at home at the booth next to Madame Vadama. The sign read: *Chakra Tuning*.

I stared at Sheridan.

"Dave, chakras are energy centers that guide our mental, physical, emotional, and spiritual well-being."

"I'm not sure I need a tune-up."

"Dave, we all need a tune-up."

The walls were hung with diagrams and pictures illustrating the chakras' locations in the body. As with the House of Living Dreams, part of the booth was partitioned off. I guessed that was where the tuning took place. Or maybe the napping.

"A pleasant evening to you," I said to a dark-haired, middle-aged man with a bit of a paunch.

"Greetings, I hope all is well with you gentlemen."

"Has been so far. I'm Sheridan and this is Dave. We're helping out in Eve's Garden."

"Ah, yes. I've seen the lovely plants. Their presence is a gift. I am Rajiv. It is a pleasure to meet you."

"It's good to meet you as well. I'll be sure to relay to Eve what you said about the plants. They may be a gift but carrying them in here wasn't."

"It is the gift of giving. You have honored the plants."

"They'd rather be getting filtered morning light at home, but it's kind of you to hold it that way."

"I'd be honored to tune your chakras so you and the plants will be aligned."

"Let me get back to you on that. We're taking a tour and getting acquainted with the place."

I could see there might be a shift in my usual conversations. While Rajiv was polite and well-spoken, I figured him for a bit of a hustler too. I imagined the chakra tuning wouldn't be a free gift.

Next up was Spirit Cassandra Astrological Readings. Charts and pictures of the solar system lined the walls. And by a small circular table draped with a purple velvet cloth were two chairs. Both empty. We turned back. I peered into Aladdin's Journey—lots of candles, incense, stones etched with maxims of one sort or another, and Ouija boards. But no live bodies there either. Which was fine because the booth that held the most interest for me was the one between Aladdin's Journey and Eve's Garden. The sign read: *The Love Doctor.*

Two comfortable-looking chairs. A small table. And a stack of business cards.

Nothing else. The Love Doctor, it seemed, was sharing their love elsewhere. I'd have to be patient—not my strongest suit.

CHAPTER EIGHT

Forces at Play

WE GOT BACK to the Garden, and Eve asked me if I'd hold down the fort while she and Sheridan got something to eat. Eve had yet to put prices on anything so, for the time being, I wouldn't conduct any sales; if someone was interested, I was to inform them that she'd be back soon.

There's a part of me that would have preferred to sit at the back and keep a low profile. There's another part of me that enjoys watching a parade. I brought one of the stools up to the front.

Some vendors, who were likely done setting up, were strolling and taking in their counterparts and what they had to offer. Dr. Ketchall was still unpacking and labeling items. Madame Vadama and her friends were chatting, and Rajiv was sitting cross-legged on the floor, seemingly lost in his chakras. This was the New Age, or so it said in my brochure—the Age of Aquarius—and people were questing for universal knowledge, holistic healing, expanding consciousness, and who knew what else. The highway was endless and tomorrow we'd discover who would drive down, up, over, and through it.

A commotion erupted nearby and people began running to the other side of the UFO booth. I was curious about what was occurring but didn't want to abandon my post. I have military training, such as it was, and it was drilled into me that when you're supposed to be standing watch, you're supposed to be standing watch.

That didn't mean I couldn't move twenty feet and find out what was happening while keeping an eye on Eve's.

The booth was only partially set up. A man lay on the floor beside the *Tantric Sex* sign. A woman was trying to resuscitate him, but he looked like he wasn't going anywhere.

The longer he remained motionless, the bigger the crowd. Five minutes later, the paramedics and the police arrived, and the guy was removed from the premises. Left behind were two visibly upset women, two trying-to-be-empathetic police officers, and the crowd of onlookers.

The forces that worried Eve had announced their arrival and now it was my job to try to stop them. I wanted to talk to the two women, but the police were keeping them occupied. I opted for the UFOs instead.

There were two of them. I'd already met some of the other neighbors, and names have a way of being heard and then lost in the deeper recesses of my universe. I'll call them One and Two. One was in his late twenties and had a sallow, lonely look about him. Two appeared to be older by ten years, around my age.

"Hey, fellas. How you doing? I'm working over at Eve's Garden. This is horrible. Do you have any idea what happened?"

"Of course we do. We're to blame. As soon as the police finish with Candy and Saffron, we'll speak to them."

"That's honorable of you. Not everyone would step forward."

"We warned Gordon. But he wouldn't listen. Few do."

"I hear you. What did you tell him?"

"We told him not to touch us. He said we were resisting the love and tried to hug us. It killed him."

"Hugging you killed him?"

"We didn't let him hug us, but he touched us. That's what killed him."

"Touching you will kill someone?"

"Yes. We get it. You don't believe us. The police won't either. But you wait. If anyone else touches us, there'll be more bodies."

CHAPTER NINE

What Do You Believe?

I KNOW THERE'S a lot of this New Age woo-woo stuff you don't believe. I'm right there with you.

Touch someone and die? I don't think so. People have infectious diseases, and who knows what kind of pollutants are poisoning us, but the anti-Midas touch? Nah, I couldn't believe that.

Of course, what you believe and what you do aren't always aligned. I had no intention of touching the UFOs, and hoped others would heed their advice.

"It's happening. I told you," Eve said.

"Yes, you did. The forces are stirred up. Do you honestly think those UFO guys killed that guy by touching him?"

"Dave," Sheridan said, "the forces are mysterious, but those boys are space cadets."

"Does that mean they have the killing touch?"

"No, Dave. They don't have the touch, but they've been touched."

"The forces will manifest themselves in various ways," Eve said. "It's possible they've been exposed to something poisonous and spread it, but most likely it was something else that killed that man."

"Are forces kind of like chakras in that they're energy masses?"

"Yes, but the chakras are in us. The forces are in the universe and they can enter us."

"Sort of like when I have an uncontrollable urge to have ice cream?"

"No, Dave. What Eve is trying to convey to you is that you can have an urge for ice cream and be driven to get some, but you can resist."

"Not that often."

"You can't resist the forces. They run their own course."

"I'm sure. But I'm a meat-and-potatoes guy, although I'm trying to cut down on the meat. I sort of have to see things to believe them."

"Well, you saw that dead guy. If that doesn't convince you, perhaps this will."

He gawked over my shoulder. We all turned.

"Hello," said a vision before me. "I'm Nova, the Love Doctor."

CHAPTER TEN

The Love Doctor Is In

BEAUTY IS IN the eye of the beholder. What we behold on the outside does not necessarily translate to the inside. That said, Nova was a knockout. Some men and women have looks that steal the room. Doesn't matter what's going on, when they come in, all eyes are on them.

While I'm sure many of us wouldn't mind having those looks, you can bet they come with a price. You and I might lament a lack of attention, but relative anonymity has its benefits. The Love Doctor couldn't go anywhere without someone staring at her, approaching her, and annoying her.

I got in the queue.

She was wearing jeans, a white T-shirt, and a dark-blue blazer. Auburn hair curled halfway down her back, and her cheek bones highlighted sparkling dark-gray eyes. And that smile? It was an invitation. At least, that's how I chose to read it.

"I'm sorry, I just got here," she said. "My booth is next door. There's distress in the air. What's going on?"

"Welcome. I'm Eve. This is Sheridan and David. And, yes, something horrible has happened. One of the men in the tantric-sex booth just collapsed and died."

"Oh, that's terrible. No wonder people are upset."

Sheridan nodded toward the UFO guys. "If you go over that way, you might want to avoid contact with those gentlemen."

"Why's that?"

"According to them," I said, "they killed him. Apparently, they're not good to the touch."

"Good to the touch? What does that mean? And why are they still here if they killed him?"

"While they're positive they killed the man," said Sheridan, "others don't agree."

"I don't understand."

"Join the club," I said, trying to get her in a joining mood. "Evidently, they've been on an interstellar vacation and caught something that will kill you if you touch them."

"I've heard of that."

"You have?" we all said.

"You go to enough of these expos, you meet them all. I'm assuming you're first-timers."

"Are we that obvious?" Eve asked.

"No, your booth is lovely and there's nothing wrong with being a first-timer. My presence at these is more questionable."

"Your booth sign piqued my interest," Eve said. "Can you tell us about being the Love Doctor?"

"It's a marketing thing. I used to call myself a personal consultant, but that didn't garner any attention. A few friends were hanging out one night and someone suggested I call myself the Love Doctor. I got business cards, the poster, and the red curtains, and ta-dah!"

"And pray tell," said Eve, "what does the Love Doctor do? I may need to come over."

"I'm a therapist type, but I can't legally use that word. I have a master's in counseling psychology, but no license. You don't need a license to be the Love Doctor. Just chutzpah."

"Bravo for you," said Eve.

"Thank you."

"If I come and share my relationship challenges," Eve said, staring at Sheridan, "could you give me some pointers?"

"Come and find out. The first five minutes is free."

I'd have liked a free five minutes with Nova but I had another appointment.

CHAPTER ELEVEN

Seems Like Old Times

I WAS MAKING my way through the parking lot when I heard, "What the fuck took you so long?"

Bennett hurried over to me.

And he wasn't alone.

"Jesus Christ. Those fuckers wouldn't let me in there. Only the people who are working the show are allowed in tonight. I've had to cool my ass out here for the past couple of hours."

"Louise. Lucky. How nice see you," I said. "I see you brought your pal."

Louise gave me the kind of hug that made me want to hug her more. Her close-to-six-foot rugby-player frame was adorned with a shorter-than-short miniskirt and an extremely enhanced chest. Long blonde hair cascaded over her shoulders. If you're just meeting her, Louise runs a brothel in Vegas when Bennett isn't paying for house calls. Like me, she works out of the box.

Lucky gave me a hearty hug with no slaps on the back. I'd met him in Vegas too; Bulgarian-born, he was my cab driver back when driving cabs was how he made his living. Currently, he was in the sleuth business himself, thanks to an unexpected cash infusion. He'd helped me out a time or two, and Bennett also employed him periodically for security concerns.

"What about me? Don't I get a fucking hug?" Bennett said.

He wrapped me up and lifted me off the ground. He's taller and heavier than me so that wasn't exactly a major accomplishment; neither was it a welcome one. I don't hug clients unless they want to hug me. I've come to appreciate hugging, yet prefer it without the air lift.

"Now that we got that out of the way, we gotta talk."

That's something I like about Bennett—he pretty much goes toe to toe with me in skipping foreplay.

"As you can see," I said, "I'm on my way to my car so I can go home, feed and walk the dog, go to sleep, and come back tomorrow."

"We all need to eat and sleep. But, for now, we have larger concerns."

"We do?"

"Yes, we do. Don't be playing cutesy with me. You know you're going to help me out. Why dick around?"

"My intention wasn't to dick around. It's just that your priorities are not always mine. We all have our own lives."

"Dave, come on. Do we have to play this game? I'm here. You're here. Louise and Lucky are here. We got the team together. Don't you want to know what we're going to do?"

"Let me guess. Does it have to do with ingesting massive amounts of cocaine and fucking your brains out?"

"Of course. At least, that's what I'll be doing. But let's not play the obvious card."

"Okay, why don't you play the less obvious one."

"We need a plan. Louise and Lucky say I'm going too far. You know me. I don't do limits. I do excess."

"I've learned that about you. But if Louise and Lucky say you're pushing it too far, most likely I'm going to agree with them."

"Yes, yes. Of course you will. But that won't stop you. We have to get those fuckers off my back."

"I gather we're talking about Mr. Russo and Caddy, who'll cut you off if they find out you're doing coke."

If you haven't read *A Lesson in Comedy and Murder*, Caddy is the name I assigned to the number-two guy. Mr. Russo was number one, the alpha—the money-fronting, no-nonsense, and connected producer of Bennett's movie.

"Let's not talk history. Let's make history. Let's fuck them over first."

"You're right. I'm with Louise and Lucky. I don't think it's prudent to fuck with them. If you want to do the coke and fuck Louise and hookers, just give up the money or locate a couple of hookers you can trust."

"That isn't going to happen," Lucky said.

"We need a fucking plan," Bennett said. "I've made it easy for you. I got you a room at the Miramar. We're all staying there over the weekend."

"Thanks, but I don't need to stay there. My home is a half hour away and my new dog, Winnie, while quite self-sufficient, won't take kindly to me being gone for an extended period of time."

"Lucky can go over there and take care of the dog. Let's not let small details get in the way. We have bigger things to do."

"My dog would not appreciate being called a small detail. She's a St. Bernard who I recently inherited and of whom I've grown quite fond. And if Lucky meets her, I'm sure he'll agree."

"Boys, here's what we'll do," Louise said. "We'll go to the Miramar and I'll make sure Bennie behaves. Doc, why don't you go home, take care of Winnie, and get a full night's sleep? We'll drop by tomorrow."

The woman had a way of getting things done, I'll give her that. I grabbed the hall pass before Bennett could protest, and headed home.

CHAPTER TWELVE

No Touching

Thursday, August 8, 1985

I HAVE A colleague whom I sometimes consult with regarding Bennett, while protecting his anonymity. She wishes I'd stop working with him and she's used some unbecoming words to describe him. I bet that when she hears what Bennett said to me, well, she'll be fuming. She'd have told him off and been done with him.

But I'm not her. Don't get me wrong. I'm not a complete pushover; I can stand up for myself. But the truth is I get a kick out of Bennett. I can't act like the kind of asshole he is. I don't have any friends who act like him. Yet I do admire how he seizes power. And he does have a good heart and, as much as he likes acting out, he lets Louise boss him around. She's a dominatrix, by the way.

Plus, it doesn't hurt that I get well paid for helping him out. Would I prefer it if he behaved better? Certainly, but he hasn't been my client that long and he's definitely a candidate for long-term therapy.

I've been unable to come up with a comprehensive job description that explains my out-of-the-box work. For the comedy conference, I had to sign a contract that had this all-inclusive phrase—*Other duties as assigned.* That sort of covers it.

So here I was. Bennett wanted me to get Mr. Russo and Caddy off his back and Eve wanted me to counter the negative forces in play—I'd call those other duties as assigned. I hadn't been able to quell those forces before they'd had their way, but hopefully I'd stop them before they doubled down.

After checking in with Eve and Sheridan, I decided to talk with our interstellar travelers. I don't usually relish the idea of poring over pictures of other people's vacations, but theirs piqued my interest. Just as long as I didn't touch them.

The lanyard got me through the doors before ten. Madame Vadama waved, Dr. Ketchall nodded, and Rajiv bowed. Aside from last-minute tidying up, everyone was ready and waiting.

Except Nova.

Being a guy who considers being on time to marginally border being late, I had concerns.

"Hey, guys," I said to One and Two. "How you doing?"

"We're fine," One said. "Still freaked by Gordon dying. We've been exceedingly clear and straightforward about the touching. Look," he said, pointing to a sign I hadn't noticed before. "Read the sign. It says: DO NOT TOUCH US. IT WILL KILL YOU. We couldn't be clearer, but people think we're full of it. It's very troubling when this happens."

"When this happens?"

"Well, this isn't the first time. We tell the police. They laugh at us and tell us they'll lock us up if we make trouble. *We make trouble?* We don't want to make trouble. We just want to talk about our vacation."

"I'm interested in your vacation and why you're poisonous to the touch. Please feel free to tell me."

"Read the other sign," Two said, pointing at it.

It said: *HEAR THE STORY—$10.*

"Ah. Yes. That must be quite a story."

"We lived to tell it."

And sell it.

"Congratulations. I don't have time now. Perhaps later. Before I go, I have a question for you. How long after you touched that guy did he die?"

"Around an hour," One said. "It doesn't take long."

"So after he touched you, did he go back to the booth and did you see him there? Was there anything unusual?"

"There were people going in and out," Two said. "And lots of loud noises."

One nodded. "Yeah. It was weird. Kind of like chanting but I've never heard anything like it. Maybe it was a religious-ecstasy thing."

"Religious ecstasy is a thing?"

"All ecstasy is a thing."

Things don't get much better than ecstasy. I don't have much experience with it, but I imagine it's awfully intense.

CHAPTER THIRTEEN

Tantric-Sex Booth

IF WE COULD pick the moment when we die, some of us would opt to go out in a moment of ecstasy. For all we know, that last moment is one of ecstasy. Who knows?

In a moment of ecstasy, one could die from any number of things. Being touched an hour beforehand was one option. Another and more likely scenario was that someone else's hand had been at play. I'd keep an open mind and see where my kiss-of-death list took me.

I said goodbye to the UFOs and headed over to the tantric-sex booth. The police had released the scene and the remaining team had wasted no time in making it more inviting with the addition of a small couch and some chairs, along with some billowing soft-colored fabrics. The back half of the booth was portioned off. That seemed to be a thing, and it made sense. There was no privacy to be had with the open floor plan; having a closed-off space was something I wished Eve had looped in.

I'd been to a conference for sex therapists and surrogates, and learned about tantric sex. There's a lot of breathing and meditation, and no direct emphasis on sex. Things start slow and build to an orgasmic state. I'm not much of a slow starter so it's never worked for me, but it has for others.

The two women I'd seen before were in the booth. One had long blonde hair. She was shapely and dressed all in white. The other was a brunette, and I was struck by the intensity of her eyes. She was all in purple. For the moment, neither appeared interested in tantric sex. They had company—a man I hadn't seen before. Good-looking, well-built, and I imagine tantrically inclined. All three were sitting on a couch.

"Hi, I'm David. I'm down a couple of booths—Eve's Garden. I wanted to come by and offer my condolences. It's a horrible thing that befell your colleague and I'm sure having to carrying on is not easy."

The blond displayed a stoic smile that might have been genuine. "Yes, but we're here. I'm Candy and this is Saffron and Phillippe."

"Pleased to meet you. Have you all been colleagues for a long time?"

"We've been in business together for a couple of years so losing Gordon is a huge loss."

"I'm sorry to hear that."

"It is sad," Saffron said, "but with every loss there's gain."

"That's true, yet sometimes it's hard to see at first."

"We see it," Phillippe said.

"Oh?"

"It's not a secret," Candy said. "We're business partners. Having one less partner increases our share."

"Yeah, I see that—the loss and the gain. I heard there was chanting or religious-ecstasy noises before he died. What was that?"

Saffron smiled. "We were warming up."

CHAPTER FOURTEEN

The Doctor Is In

I WOULD HAVE liked to linger with the tantric-sexers, but the doors were opening soon and I wanted to try to make a connection with Nova before the horde came in.

She was sitting comfortably in one of the two chairs, watching the traffic. Her face lit up a bit when she saw me and all the blood in my body rushed to my face as I beamed too broadly at her.

"Hi, I'm glad you're here. I was hoping to have a moment with you before things get busy."

"Good morning. It's good to see you," Nova said.

"Yes, it's good to see you as well. And good morning. Listen, I might as well tell you now, I'm not very good at foreplay..."

"This is foreplay?"

"Well, I hope so, but like I said, I'm not good at it. Not that it doesn't excite me. It's just that when I'm overly nervous my mind, body, and spirit definitely do not align well. How was that for a beginning? Okay?"

"So, you'd prefer to start our relationship at third base?"

"I was going to go for second, but I'd be happy to start at third. You want to start there?"

"I'd go for starting before the part where they sing the anthem and go out on the field. How does that sound to you?"

"I'd be getting my hot dogs then so that works. I appreciate the baseball analogies. Not long ago, I attended the Dodgers Adult Fantasy Baseball Camp and since then I've upped my usage of baseball references. The fact that you used them makes it real hard to start at the part before the anthem."

That's when a couple of women in their twenties came up to the booth and asked if she was the Love Doctor.

She glanced at me and winked.

And I got excited.

CHAPTER FIFTEEN

Walking the Beat

I HADN'T GOTTEN to third base with Nova, but neither had I been thrown out of the game. We were still waiting for them to sing the anthem, although I think that wink meant "Play ball."

I get that she has to be cautious when it comes to relationships; a lot of people are probably drawn to her solely for her beauty. I was. It's an easy thing to be attracted to, and so it made sense that she'd want someone to run the bases so she could be sure they were genuinely interested in her and not just the vision.

I'd made the mistake before of being attracted to someone for their beauty and found out later there were less appealing things bubbling below the surface. It would be wise for me to slow things down and get a clearer view of who she was as opposed to who I wanted her to be. Talking that talk was one thing though; looking at her was another, and made it harder to walk.

Plus, before I could walk anywhere with Nova, I needed to spend time exploring the expo; try to ascertain what was stoking the forces and what I'd need to do to put them out.

Business was picking up for Madame Vadama and Dr. Ketchall, but Rajiv seemed to need a tune-up. Given that he was across from Nova, I thought I'd see what I could do.

Before I could see anything there was an announcement over a loudspeaker. There would be an on-stage demonstration of tarot-card reading in five minutes. I went across the aisle.

"Good morning. I don't mean to be rude, but are you all right? Have you been spending time over at the UFO booth?"

"Good morning to you as well. I'd be pleased to go over there, but I'm too upset."

"What's the matter?"

"It's my sacral chakra. I can't balance it. I know I'm being hard on myself but since that gentleman died I have not been myself."

"It's disconcerting to have someone die so close to you."

"Yes, it is quite disturbing. However, I must confess I'm not as bothered by his death as I am by how it has affected me."

"It's hard to allow yourself to be lighthearted in the face of death."

"It's not that. My anahata chakra, my heart chakra, is fine. I have compassion for the man and those close to him. He was a devotee of tantric sex, as am I. Yet since his death I do not feel deserving of pleasure."

"That's disheartening."

"I need to open the pathway. If I could do that, customers would come and I'd make some money. I cannot afford to be here and be out of balance."

"I hear you. Not an ideal time to be out of balance. Is there something I can do to help?"

"I've been doing the goddess pose, which usually unblocks me, but not today. I tried to dance to the music the astrologer next door is playing but, alas, that too is not working. The forces are against me. I'm destined to be this way for now."

"Yes, you are. Doing those things to try to move your energy is worth the effort, but here's what I've learned. Acceptance. Rather than trying to remove the blockage, why not accept that it's here now? It will leave, hopefully soon, but maybe you need not concern yourself with being other than you are in this moment."

Rajiv examined me with surprise, perhaps even a hint of respect, then nodded, bid me adieu, and stepped behind his curtain.

I strolled down the aisle and got a Lean, Mean, Green Bean smoothie that sounded better than it tasted. I window-shopped down the aisle until I got to the end and threw it out. It might be healthy, but I couldn't stomach it.

I peeked back up to Rajiv's booth. He was out front, pacing. Maybe his tried and true chakra-balancing techniques weren't getting the job done, and my suggestion of acceptance wasn't helping.

I turned my attention to the booth at the end of the aisle.

Ever heard of primal-scream therapy? Back in the seventies, it had its fifteen minutes of fame. I know less about it than I do chakras but as far as I could tell, you went into a soundproof telephone booth type of structure and screamed.

End of therapy.

So many of us keep things bottled up that it's helpful to let off steam once in a while. Being in LA, I tell clients to park their car in a quiet location and scream their head off until they're ready to go. It's usually relieving and can be invigorating. It might be called for after a Lean, Mean, Green Bean smoothie.

I swung by Rajiv's again. Had he still been in a funk, I'd have suggested it—the primal-scream therapy, not the smoothie—but things had picked up.

There was a line to speak with the Love Doctor. I wouldn't have minded so much if most of them hadn't been guys. It seemed my own chakras were getting out of balance.

Then something caught my eye.

CHAPTER SIXTEEN

Guess Who I Just Saw

YOU KNOW WHEN you see something but then, later, you're not convinced that what you saw is what you saw? You get a glimpse, but before you can fully register it, it disappears. That's what had caught my eye—something… no, someone familiar but unreachable in that moment. It was both balancing and unbalancing.

I was trying to figure out what I'd seen when a voice interrupted me.

"At last. This place is packed with kooks."

"Good morning, Bennett," I said. "It's kind of early for you to be up and out."

"Dave, time doesn't exist when I'm with Louise. We've been up all night and she's enthralled me in ways I only wish I could remember. But we have a problem and you need to fix it."

"Thank you for your confidence in me, but while it may not appear that I'm working, I am."

"You call moping around like someone stole your favorite toy working?"

"Honey, don't beat up on Doc. Can't you see he's pining for the Love Doctor?" Louise said as she hugged me.

"She's a looker," Bennett said. "Not in your category, but if you're going to pine for someone, she looks worth it."

"You're not alone," Lucky said. "She draws them in like an early-bird special."

"She's probably out of my league, but she did throw out some baseball metaphors so maybe I have a chance."

"That's great, Dave, but can we focus? You need to help me out. You're the doctor. Do your medicine. Make things better."

"I'm the kind of doctor that advocates for his clients taking responsibility for their lives."

"If I did that, I wouldn't need you. Now, quit this dicking around and get to work."

"I don't consider it dicking around when I encourage you to take responsibility for your life."

"Stop it, Dave. I'm taking responsibility. I'm speaking with you. I can't do everything. It pains me to admit it, yet it's true. I have my failings and hire others to help me out. So help me out."

"Okay. Let me see what I can do. But I have to tell you, you have problems."

"That's what I just said. I hired you to help me with my problems."

"So let me help you. Don't turn. Don't move. Stare at me and let me share with you what I just glimpsed out of the corner of my eye."

Of course, Bennett turned and surveyed the premises.

But that was okay. He wasn't there anymore.

Rip, I mean.

That was the wisp of something I thought I'd seen.

It was confirmed when I caught another glimpse of him at the end of the aisle.

"What am I looking for?" Bennett said. "UFO freaks, tantric-sex practitioners, clairvoyants, and herbalists? There's no shortage of weird people here. The crowd at the mystery conference was weird enough, but this group takes the cake."

"We've got lots of different world views in attendance," I said.

"But that's not what I wanted to point out. There's someone here whose presence means you need to be extremely careful."

"What do you mean? Who's here?"

"It's Rip. He's following you."

"Who's Rip?"

"Lucky, why don't you tell him."

"Rip is employed by Mr. Russo. He was in Doc's group at the comedy conference and Doc kind of got him interested in psychology. Sort of like my sister's husband's brother who sells cars and got religion and now wants to be telling the truth."

"What?"

"What Lucky is saying is that Rip is likely here because Mr. Russo and Caddy told him to follow you and catch you doing coke. What that has to do with selling cars and telling the truth, I have no idea."

"You can't sell cars and tell the truth. If my sister's husband's brother starts telling the truth too much he'll lose his job."

"What the fuck? They're following me? I'm fucked. My life is going to shit and no one is helping."

"Bennie, slow down," Louise said. "We're trying to help you. If Rip is following you, you need to make sure he doesn't follow you to the hotel."

"It's too late for that," Lucky said.

"Yeah, if you're planning on giving him the slip, which I'd encourage, then go to a different hotel. And get someone he won't recognize to go pick up your stuff."

"Lucky said Rip was influenced by you. Can't you get him to back off?"

"I can't do that. But why don't you and Louise make the rounds and raise your consciousness? Lucky can try to follow Rip. When Rip takes a bathroom break, Lucky can beep you and you can dash out to the parking lot and head for a new hotel."

Two jobs. More forces in play. This wouldn't be easy.

CHAPTER SEVENTEEN
The Future

"I HAVE TO speak with you," Eve whispered, and pulled me to one side of the two customers she'd been attending to. "Don't go away. As soon as I have a moment I need to explain something."

"I'll wait here."

I waited and watched. Madame Vadama waved me over.

"Dr. Unger, you haven't come to see me. Why is that? You know I've seen your future."

"Yes, you mentioned my afterlife. Do you see anything a little closer to the moment?"

"I see it all, yet I do not tell it all. Madame cannot make a living that way."

"How about: do you see anything in the near future romance-wise? How about that?"

"You do not give for free what people most want."

"What *are* you giving for free this morning?"

"You are fortunate. I'm in a generous mood. Eve told me I needed to do right by you, so I will tell you one thing. But if you want more you must pay."

"That's fair. What have you got?"

"Madame Vadama does see romance." A smile played ever so slightly on her face. "But it is not what you think."

"Hi, will you be my partner?"

"You're even less into foreplay than I am. Are we talking tantric sex? In which case, you'd be better served picking someone else. In case you forgot, my name is David."

"Thanks. I did forget. I remembered you, but not your name."

"I usually forget names, but I remembered yours."

"Most do. That's why I use it for business."

"So we'll be conducting business?"

"We'll be demonstrating nurturing meditation. Since you don't know what you're doing, you'll be the receiver and I the giver."

"Okay. Although I tend to be more of a giver than a receiver."

"All the more reason. Come on, let's go."

Left to my own devices, I'd have skipped the first steps on the path to tantric sex. Nurturing meditation sounded like foreplay to me. Not that either is a bad thing; it's just that I tend to gloss over those stages. The fact that I see it as a step toward someplace precludes me from valuing it much in and of itself. I can say that, and endeavor to value each thing within itself, yet I'd still want to rush through it to get to those more exciting stages. Then I'd want to slow down, but might not be able to.

It would be beneficial for me to be the receiver, even though it made me uneasy. It's not that I don't enjoy being on the receiving end; it's that I usually spend too much time worrying about reciprocating. Maybe with Candy there wouldn't be any IOUs, but free gifts usually come with small print.

There were half a dozen curious onlookers standing around a mat on the floor, listening to Phillippe describe what Candy and I were about to do. I felt extremely uncomfortable. I'm not one for being on display, especially when what I'm displaying is my ineptitude.

We lay down in the spoon position, me on the receiving end. Phillippe narrated.

The good news was I wasn't fretting about reciprocating. The bad news was I was fretting about becoming aroused. While that

CHAPTER EIGHTEEN
We're Disturbed

YOU EVER SEE someone and think you've met them before but can't place their face? Living in LA, sometimes I see someone and wonder whether I really do know them or they're someone I've seen in a movie or on TV.

A woman came up to Madame Vadama and hugged her briefly. Mid-twenties. Blonde. Cold-looking. Good-looking. I'd seen her before but couldn't recall where or when. She didn't acknowledge me. I'm used to being ignored, but people I know usually say hello.

Madame Vadama escorted her behind the curtain. It bothered me that I couldn't pull her face out of my memory bank. It would probably come to me in the middle of the night. I'd worry about remembering, consider writing it down, resolve to remember it, and by morning have forgotten but remember I'd determined to remember.

I felt a tap on my shoulder.

"There's trouble," Eve said. "I see it. It's all around us."

"You mean like pollution?"

"No. Yes. Like that, but worse."

"Politics?"

"Not that bad. But worse."

"Is this the forces?"

"I can see it. Your aura, my aura, Sheridan, the UFO lot, the tantric-sexers, Dr. Ketchall, Madame Vadama, Nova. They're all disturbed."

"Our auras are disturbed? What does that mean?"

"We're all dark, gray, black. It's horrible. You can't trust anyone or anything."

"That's disturbing. I take it you're a big believer in auras."

"Don't say it like that. Many of us have tapped into sources that others haven't accessed, but that doesn't mean they're not real. Just because you can't see auras doesn't mean others can't. I can teach you to see them, although not everyone can."

"I'm here to learn so maybe another time you could teach me. I didn't mean to be overly cynical. If you believe in them, they're real for you. Your sense of things has certainly been attuned so far, so I'm paying attention. But if I'm going to trust what you say about not trusting anyone, I'm going to have to include you in that."

"Of course."

Things were not getting easier.

CHAPTER NINETEEN
Nurturing Meditation

SEEING IS BELIEVING. That's something I used to believe. The some things and it turned out that what I was seeing wasn't was seeing. I'd just taken for granted that it was. Sort of like mirage or dream is real until it isn't.

Eve felt forces and saw auras. Madame Vadama saw the Rajiv tuned your chakras even if he couldn't tune his. I'm n any of those things are real, but I do know that if you believe thing to be true, it's true for you.

As for my own sense of what was and wasn't real, that f reliable. When you can't trust anyone or anything, it messe your mind, and mine is messy enough to begin with.

After I left Eve, I thought of what I ought to have asked how far did those disturbing auras extend? Were they locali was the whole expo out of balance?

I'm a big believer in trusting yourself. When you get dowr what else have you got? Partial truths, people who serve thei interests before yours, and the fickle finger of fate. I wasn't rea trust that I was untrustworthy, even though I was fully cogniza the fact that I hadn't always made the best decisions.

Candy approached me and my trust antenna wiggled.

might have driven viewer interest and pleased Candy, I focused on the Dodgers' batting order. It didn't put me in the kind of headspace Candy was wanting, but it did the trick.

Phillippe told us to snuggle up chakra to chakra. Candy snuggled up well and I tried to recall the names of the kids in my eighth-grade class. Her left arm slid under my neck and her hand rested on my forehead. That was fine. Her right arm came over me and her hand pressed up against my heart. I was glad I'd been asked to go on the receiving end.

Phillippe instructed us to synchronize our breath. I was grateful for that as it gave me yet another thing to concentrate on. As I inhaled, he told me to open myself to receiving Candy's chakra energy, and as she exhaled to focus on releasing it. I decided I'd be better off focusing on the breathing.

The audience was told that when they did this at home they could add a second technique which would be demonstrated at one o'clock.

Candy and I got token applause and people came up to Phillippe. Candy touched my shoulder, thanked me, and moved over to the group. It wasn't that I begrudged her answering their questions; it was just that after having received what she was giving, I wanted more.

CHAPTER TWENTY
Aura Check

MADAME VADAMA HAD said romance was in my future but not in the way I'd thought. I'd been hoping for romance with Nova but was I in store for some with Candy? What I'd lose in love, I might gain in sex. There have been times when I wouldn't have minded the trade-off, but I was coming to a place in my life where great sex was, indeed, great sex, but great love would get my vote, especially if it included great sex. Plus, great sex with Candy would include an abundance of foreplay, which while likely rewarding for me, wouldn't come easily.

But I could be motivated to try. I was contemplating where the forces would take me when Eve waved me over.

"Will you please watch the booth while we get lunch?"

"Happy to. If someone wants something, I'll tell them you'll be back soon."

"Perfect. Or you can sell them something if they don't want to wait. If Samuel comes by, Sheridan left a package for him under one of the stools."

She headed off and I held my position until I couldn't keep my curiosity in check any longer. I took a peek inside Samuel's package.

Evidently, the harvest from Eve's Garden could be smoked and inhaled.

Samuel didn't come by to pick up his stash, but a couple of other guys showed up asking for Sheridan and I told them he'd be back soon. Even if Eve's part of the Garden wasn't making ends meet, it seemed that Sheridan's medicinal aids were faring well.

Sheridan was first back. "Dave, Eve needs to speak with you."

"All right. By the way, a couple of guys dropped by. I told them you'd be back soon."

"Were they grumpy?"

"Not to me."

"That's a relief. I told my regulars I'd be here all week so they've had to pay the admission to get in. I've heard grumbling."

"Yeah, well, tell them to go exploring. It's a head trip being here. They should be thanking you."

"I'll tell them you said that."

"Yeah. Just reframe their grumbling as an opportunity. We shrinks do that all the time. It even has a name—reframing."

"We dealers have a name for it too—bullshit."

"Yeah, well, there's a lot of bullshit in the healing professions. In all professions, I guess."

"I have bad news," Eve said. "Well, it isn't bad for everyone else."

"I guess that's good for them."

"I was checking out auras over lunch."

"Makes sense. Did you notice that when you left our disturbed zone here, your aura lifted?"

"Sadly, ours remained the same. And everyone else is clear. It's not about being at the expo. It's something about us."

CHAPTER TWENTY-ONE
Talking the Walk

IF WE ARE the architects of our lives, we also need to be the designers and builders. I keep building similar structures. The books I write start the same, end the same, and pretty much are the same. You could frame that different ways depending on your mood.

I rely on the familiar. I like the comfort of the known. I like to do things my way. If I was going to solve this whodunit, I'd need to do it my way—by focusing on our disturbed-aura group and using its forces to dislodge the culprit.

And therein lay the challenge, because the members of our disturbed group weren't clued in to the idea that we were a group. Furthermore, while I knew there was a group, I wasn't exactly clear who was in it. I'd need for Eve to instruct me, and periodically check everyone out to see how we were hueing.

Eve had already identified Nova as being part of the group, so why not employ my investigative powers with her as a starting point? I could investigate what might have caused her disturbance. Truthfully, I wanted to see if she was up for playing some more ball.

I was ready for lunch. Maybe she was too.

Two guys who were marginally better looking than me were speaking with her. Well, more like flirting with her. I stood on the periphery and pretended not to listen while trying to get a sense of whether they were getting any further than I had.

I managed to hear a few words—*real estate, malpractice, anonymous*. Not flirting words per se, but context is everything.

Eventually they left. I gave it a moment and approached her.

"I saw you there," Nova said. "I was wondering if you were planning on interrupting."

"If you ever want me to, pull on your ear lobe and I'll barge in."

"Will do."

"I'm going to lunch and would welcome your company."

"That's very kind. Unfortunately, I've got someone coming soon."

"Too bad. I was hoping we'd spend some time together and determine if we're interested in continuing to spend time together. I'm pretty sure I am, but I'm trying not to rush into things. I just want to see if we can get the ball rolling."

"So I gather. You interested in dinner?"

"Now you've done it. I'll try to stay in the moment and not get ahead of myself, but I already am."

"Given how self-aware you are, I'd have thought you'd be able to do something about that."

"You'd think so. I mostly attend to the here and now, unless I'm excited. In my defense, at least I'm talking the talk even if I'm not walking it."

"I suppose that's something. And now I have to go."

"So I'll meet you here at?"

"Let's make it seven."

And there it was, my ticket to the game.

CHAPTER TWENTY-TWO

Following

BE STILL MY heart.

Didn't Odysseus say that in Homer's *Odyssey*? The only reason I remember is because my ninth-grade English teacher, Ms. Beale, repeated it every time I managed to answer something correctly.

Nova had invited me to dinner. The anthem receded into the background; the batter was in the on-deck circle. Things were definitely moving along. Lest I forget, she'd pointed out that I ought to have been able to better manage my natural desire to push things forward. My self-management is not consistently well-balanced. Perhaps Rajiv could give whatever chakra was involved a tune-up.

I went out in the lobby and got a bad hot dog that needed a lot of mustard and relish to distract me from what I was ingesting. I was still lolling in my excitement when Candy dashed out of the front entrance. She could be leaving for any number of reasons, but since I had nothing else to do than order a second hot dog, I followed her.

She went to the parking lot. I assumed she'd be driving someplace so I ran to my car, saw her leaving the lot, and took off after her. We've all seen movies where high-level following skills have been demonstrated. That's not what was on display here.

When I follow someone, I depend on their not looking behind

them. It's actually not as bad a strategy as it sounds. Unless you're driving over the speed limit or have over-indulged, there's not much reason to look behind you. I'm sufficiently challenged looking ahead.

Candy was in a hurry. She got onto Pico Boulevard and turned west. At Ocean, she hung a right, went a few blocks, and got on the ramp to Pacific Coast Highway, which lies under the entrance to the Santa Monica Pier—the location where tourists have an LA experience that most locals choose to avoid.

She was speeding up the coast. In case you haven't driven in that part of town, the Pacific Ocean rests on the other side of houses that are glued together yet remain out of most people's price range. Occasionally, I'd catch a glimpse of the wide beach and restless ocean beyond.

She drove twenty minutes and passed the Malibu Pier, where surfers were carrying on the tradition. After the lagoon she turned onto Malibu Road, drove a quarter mile or so, and parked in the driveway of 24148. A For Rent sign had been erected in front of the building—a coastal farmhouse-style mansion large enough to accommodate our disturbed group and still feel roomy. There was a car in the driveway, a black Mercedes with a license in a Goldman Realty frame.

Unless there was big money to be made in the tantric-sex business, Candy had other things going for her.

I parked down the street and began my stakeout. After half hour or so, she came out with another woman. They chatted, shook hands, and drove off in their separate cars. I followed Candy back to the Civic. She parked and went inside. I went to a phone booth and called Goldman Realty about the availability of 24148 Malibu Road.

It had just been rented for the weekend, I was told, but would be available Monday afternoon.

CHAPTER TWENTY-THREE
Stalking

IF YOU'RE WORKING over the weekend it's not unusual to treat yourself. Candy might have the money to lease a beach house in Malibu and it was no big deal to her. It could be more convenient than driving home.

Not that the possibility of her having that kind of money improved my opinion of her significantly, but it didn't hurt it either.

I headed inside and made my way to Eve's Garden. Candy was over in Tantric Sex, seemingly sharing the news about the Malibu shack-up with her booth mates and getting an enthusiastic response.

In the Garden, Eve was up front, mixing a brew of herbs for a ponytailed man with a T-shirt that declared *Make Love Not War*. Sheridan was sitting on a stool at the back. As I sidled up to him, the loudspeaker announced that the Star Fire Eternal Ointments demonstration would be on the stage in five minutes.

"Dave, good afternoon. We haven't seen you in a while. Have you had an adventure?"

"Perhaps. Perhaps not. I did a tantric mediation with a woman called Candy and decided to follow her."

"Dave, you shouldn't be telling me this. That kind of stalking can get you arrested."

"That's true. Stalking is not a condoned activity, and yet, when I'm sleuthing, I often end up following suspects."

"So you weren't following her to move your tantric meditation to a more active level?"

"I wouldn't mind that, but no. Since Eve told us there's a group of us with bad juju, I've been keeping an eye on us. I'm unclear why our auras are funky. Could be that there's foul play afoot, though it's unclear whether we're the players or the targets. So, I follow whomever I can and try to figure out the connections."

"What did you discover?"

"Candy rented a mansion on the beach in Malibu for the weekend."

"To enjoy a tantric weekend?"

"That's certainly a possibility, or she wants a fancy place to crash, though it's too big for just her. It's likely a business thing as I saw her talking to her partners and they were nodding their heads enthusiastically."

"Maybe there'll be some after-hours tantric activity there."

"I have what I hope will be a hot dinner date, though I'm not even officially at the plate yet. I could come to bat and then strike out. I hope not, but I'm up against major-league pitching. If I strike out early, I might take a ride and see what I can see."

"You positive you're not stalking her?"

I didn't think so, but what I think and what I do are not always aligned.

CHAPTER TWENTY-FOUR

Consequences

FOLLOWING/STALKING CANDY HAD taken up a decent portion of the afternoon but there was time to kill before my dinner with Nova. There were others in our "disturbed" group I could check in on. Madame Vadama was engaged with potential customers, Dr. Ketchall was making adjustments to someone on his chiropractic table, and Rajiv fretted as the parade went past his booth without stopping. I took a few steps out of Eve's Garden into the aisle. Nova was talking with a group of college-aged men, the UFOs were trying to persuade a teenager to fork out for their ten-dollar story, and Candy, Saffron, and Phillippe had a crowd.

None of that surprised me. What did surprise me was seeing Rip. He was standing at the end of the aisle. Judging from his expression as we made eye contact, he hadn't expected to see me either. We waved and walked toward each other. I hoped Bennett and the crew wouldn't be coming round the corner anytime soon.

"Hey, Dr. Unger, it's great to see you," Rip said, and gave me a big hug. Even if he was shorter than me, he was twice my size. Sumo-wrestler size.

"Rip, how nice to see you. I didn't expect to see you at an expo like this."

"Yeah, not many of us Koreans here, although we've got plenty of our own kooky stuff."

"How have you been? You look different than when I saw you last, and that was just a few months ago."

"No more flip-flops and Hawaiian shirts. Boss said I needed to class it up a bit."

"You look sharp."

"Thanks. It's not really my thing, but the boss is boss."

"Still employed by Mr. Russo?"

"Three years, which in this business is long term."

"Congratulations."

"I got something I've been wanting to ask you."

"What's that?"

"I'm reading your sex book. I gotta be honest, I don't understand why people read it, though I've been picking up pointers."

"There is something to be said for that. So you're curious why people like my books?"

"No, that's their problem."

"I suppose."

"My question is personal."

"Can you give me the short version now and we can follow up later?"

"Okay. It's my girlfriend. I'm having trouble with her."

"This might be more than a quick conversation. Can you swing by later when I'll have more time to talk?"

"I'm not sure. In my business you never know what's next."

"I hear you. I'm sorry you're having difficulty with your girlfriend. Anything I can help with off the bat?"

"I'm not having difficulty with her. It's me. I don't blame you, but in the book you said you have to take responsibility for yourself. If I hadn't gone to your workshop and if I hadn't started reading your book, I wouldn't be having these difficulties."

"I'm sorry to hear that. I did neglect to give you the disclaimer about therapy. Not that you're in therapy, but whenever you involve yourself with self-help it does reverberate in ways that can challenge you."

"You should have told us in the workshop. I'd have had to stay anyway, otherwise I'd have lost my job, but I'd have closed my ears more."

"Others do. I can't undo what I did, but I can try to assist you in dealing with the consequences."

"Thanks, Doc. You ought to include a disclaimer with these books, otherwise some readers are going to have difficult times without ever asking for it."

"I haven't ever considered that. I figured that with 'Lesson' in the title, and me being a shrink, readers would be up for the therapy stuff. Hopefully, they pick up enough resources to ride the waves. But now I'll consider it. Thanks for the suggestion."

"I'm happy to help you, and I hope you can help me."

So now I had three jobs. Help Rip. Help Bennett. Help the forces leave the premises. It was going to be a busy weekend.

CHAPTER TWENTY-FIVE

Read This

THERAPISTS AND OTHERS in the helping professions often assist others with issues they've not personally encountered. You can help even if you haven't had a similar experience, though it can give you a leg up with empathy if you've been there, done that. Of course, how you've been there and done that will differ from their experience, but it provides a connection.

Therapists don't advertise this, but for the most part we're a do-as-I-say group, not a do-as-I-do. I don't have the best credentials when it comes to romantic relationships as the longest one I've had is three years. But while I didn't have any long-term expertise to offer, that wouldn't stop me from trying to point Rip in a healing direction.

"I'm gonna cut to the chase cuz you don't like foreplay and I might have to leave any minute."

"Works for me."

"Here's where you fucked me up. Mr. Russo doesn't let anyone talk back to him. What he says goes. If I want to keep my job I have to do what he says or he'll get someone else to do it, and take care of me if I need taking care of. I accept that."

"Not ideal working conditions, but okay."

"In Korea, the woman at home is like the boss at work. She

makes all the rules. She takes my paycheck. Gives me an allowance. She's the boss."

"I didn't know that. And we're talking about your girlfriend? Not your wife?"

"That's another story. It's not a problem that she's the boss. I know my place and I accept it."

"Acceptance is important."

"That was before. Then I read your book. It's telling me to speak the truth. To stand up for what I want."

"Yeah. It does that."

"Well, it's fucking with me."

"Yeah, I can see that."

"So fix it."

A reasonable request. Yet one I couldn't fulfill. We therapists leave the bulk of the therapy to the client. We're just provocateurs. We rile things up and show you a way. We can talk about how you walk that path but you gotta do the legwork yourself.

"Why don't we fix it together?" I said anyway.

"Okay…"

"Although this seems like a bigger issue than we can fix standing here."

"Fair point, but you have to give me something."

"Here's a first step. Tell her you were in my workshop at the comedy conference and started reading my book. Then say you want to read her an excerpt."

"I don't think she'll be interested."

"Yeah, well, not everybody is. Pick a funny scene that she might enjoy. Maybe one where the woman shines. Try to ease her into it."

"Worth a try, I guess."

"After you've read it, ask her what she thinks. Hopefully you can discuss it and that will lead the way for a repeat. Take it a step at a time," said I, who likes to skip steps.

Like I said, I'm a do-as-I-say, not a do-as-I-do therapist.

CHAPTER TWENTY-SIX
Following Who?

I HAD NO place to go and nothing to do, aside from locating Bennett and company and warning them about Rip. I strolled back down the aisle and over to the next one. I couldn't see them. Maybe Lucky had caught sight of Rip talking to me and they'd taken off. And what about Rip? Had he come, hoping they'd show up, or was he here for some other business?

It would help if I had more answers and fewer questions, so I elected to double down on my afternoon activities. I'd followed Candy to Malibu. Where would following Rip take me?

It's hard to follow someone when they're not moving. It's also hard to follow someone who gets paid for whatever it is Rip gets paid for. I'm not privy to the job description for Muscle, but it likely includes a requirement for follower-detection skills, meaning Rip's would be a step up from Candy's.

Rip was pretending to be interested in tie-dyed T-shirts in a booth at the end of the aisle that was home to Eve's Garden and the rest of the disturbed group. I took up a spot with some people alongside the stage and listened to a thin blonde woman espousing the benefits of psychic weight loss.

I say listened; I was paying about as much attention as I had at school. So when Rip forewent the tie-dye and moved down the aisle I ditched the weight-loss approach and took off after him. He took his time but made it to the entrance. Then he hauled ass.

It sure seemed like he was following someone but it wasn't Bennett and company. I wouldn't make it to my car in time to follow him and there were no waiting cabs to rescue me. Instead, I scanned the parking lot to see who he was following.

I only got a passing glimpse but it was enough. I recognized her. Well, sort of. It was the woman I'd seen hugging Madame Vadama. But I'd yet to place her.

CHAPTER TWENTY-SEVEN
Dinner Date

I'D ONLY GONE through my mental Rolodex of places to have dinner five or six times. It didn't take long; I don't eat out that often. There were just two restaurants in the vicinity that I knew. Should I opt for a romantic bistro I'd been to with a woman who'd found the decor more interesting than me, or settle for Zucky's, the deli within walking distance? Maybe I'd take her someplace I'd never been. Maybe I'd ask her where she wanted to go. Maybe we'd take a drive and make the choice together.

Yet another example of why I hate foreplay. You don't think as much about this stuff once you're in a relationship. Or at least you don't worry about it. I wanted how I dealt with dinner to symbolize the kind of person I am. That put extra pressure on me, and when that occurs I'm not at my best.

While I brushed my teeth with water and one finger and made sure my hair looked combed, I narrowed down the list of possibilities to two different approaches. I was inclined to ask her where she wanted to go, although I'd recently read that women prefer it when men are assertive and sensitive, rather than deferential, so maybe I'd make a suggestion and ask her how she felt about it. I decided to make the final decision in the moment.

"Hey, you ready to call it a day?"

"Not completely. We're having dinner, are we not?"

"We are. I've been running options about where to go and how to approach the issue. Frankly, I'd just as soon go to Zucky's, though it's not exactly a first-date kind of place."

"More like a last-date kind of place."

"Well, I was thinking more like a been-around-the-bases-a-few-times kind of place. A place you go once you're familiar with a person."

"And you think we're familiar with each other?"

"It's a want-to-be. Since Zucky's will be where we go to break up, any place you'd presently prefer?"

"Zucky's will do."

"No no no. Really? We're breaking up already? Aw, that's not good."

"Are you moping?"

"I'm starting to, but I could wait till after dinner."

"What if I make it easy for you?"

"We're going Dutch?"

"Why don't we take a walk and find a promising place on Ocean Avenue?"

"You mean you're not breaking up with me?"

"I'm retaining that option until I know you better."

Walking down the street and into a restaurant with an unusually attractive woman is its own sociological study. Men stared at us. Women stared at us. Well, at her. Some said complimentary things in loud whispers; others said them directly to her. It was exciting, annoying, threatening, and encouraging for me. I imagined there were times it was a pain in the ass for her.

We ended up at a seafood place where, reluctantly yet wisely, I opted out of getting the lobster and settled for the bouillabaisse, which came with its own risk factors. I'm not the daintiest of eaters. When called upon, I can get the food from the plate and into my mouth without spillage, but to give myself an easier ride I ought to have opted for the salmon.

"Now that we've ordered and are looking at each other, I have to share something. I can see that your beauty brings things you must value and others that in all likelihood you wouldn't mind avoiding. At first, it kind of perked me up to be with this noticeably attractive woman—although I was plenty perked up already without that. The fact is, the attention you garnered is something I liked and didn't like. So what I'm trying to do is get a sense of what it's like to be you."

"I've certainly been able to get a sense of what it's like being you. Which I can see also has its up and downs. Yes, I'm often told I'm beautiful. And, yes, it feels good. I like how I look and I'm glad others do as well. But that's not the whole story, and for some that's all they want me to be."

"Yeah. That's upsetting. Yet, I have to admit, it's a delight to sit here and see you up close. It's quite the view. It's a shame you don't get to have the same experience. Still, I'm truly interested in learning more about you and discovering if I'm as attracted to the inside as I am to the outside."

"I admire your honesty. You fumble a lot, but you make it work for you. So, go ahead, enjoy the view. Let's take our time. I'm here. You're here. Let's see where we go."

What else can I tell you? She'd had a difficult and rebellious youth in Pasadena, but had excelled academically, stayed in school, and made a living modeling. She took a psychology class and got hooked. She was interested in nutrition, physical therapy, and alternative medicine, and wanted to bring various healing arts into her sessions. She was part therapist, part healer, part entrepreneur, and, most importantly, fully single.

We went back to the Civic Center parking lot and stood by her 1965 yellow Mustang convertible.

"I need a little help," I said. "We're about to say goodnight. Is this the time for our first kiss? If so, I'm happy to make the move. It's just easier when I'm sure the light's green."

"It's kind of you to ask, and awkward too, but I'm getting used to the awkward with you."

"That's a relief. I can wait or just seize the moment if it feels right. Up to you."

"That's very heedful of you. I'd say it's up to us and you've been forthright about putting your intentions out there. So let me put mine. I'd like to kiss you. However, I won't. First, you need to hear my intentions."

CHAPTER TWENTY-EIGHT

Intentions

YOU HAVE INTENTIONS? I guess we all do. Intention is a kind of fancy to-do list. I wouldn't have framed what I'd done with Nova as my putting out my intentions, but she had. I'd been forthcoming about my attraction to her, yet that probably happened to her more times in the day than I cared to know. I'd also told her about wanting to get to know her better and of my hope for romance. She probably heard that all too often as well.

While my intentions seemed to have passed the bar, they weren't quite being realized. Was this what Madame Vadama had meant when she said I'd have romance but not in the way I thought? Nova had different intentions. The kind that made her not want to kiss me until she'd explained herself.

That was respectful and I was more than willing to sit in the front seat of her Mustang and listen to her intentions. She wasn't. She wanted to wait.

So I said, "Can you take a peek into the future and see when that might be?"

"Soon. Not soon enough for you, but I suspect that's nothing new for you."

"Yeah, well, I'm the kind of guy who wants to be on third, yelling at the batter to get me home."

"I'll try to remember that. In the meantime, let's say goodnight."

"So can we at least kiss goodnight? Not a real kiss. Like a beginning nice-to-know-you kiss?"

"David, see you in the morning."

CHAPTER TWENTY-NINE
Morning News

Friday, August 9, 1985

I LIKE TO do things my way. You like to do things your way. Sometimes our ways will match up, sometimes they won't. Nova's way was to take her intentions home with her and wait for another day.

My intention had been to listen earnestly to hers… in the Mustang with the top down and the summer night above. Then to parlay that earnestness into some base running.

As it was, I was eating oatmeal with blueberries and a banana, and reading the *LA Times*. There were killings in South Africa, a car bomb in West Germany, Nicaraguan rebels on the move. American farmers were defaulting on loans, the baseball strike was over, and Dr. Ketchall had been killed the previous evening. Apparently from an overdose of an unknown substance.

Things were bad all over, except for in the world of baseball.

Eve and Sheridan were displaying her potions, lotions, and herbs when I arrived. When Eve saw me she said, "Phew. We're relieved to see you. When you weren't here we started to worry."

"We're you expecting me earlier? If so, I forgot. Sorry."

"No, Dave. You don't need to clock in. We were discussing

your being one of those if-you're-not-early-you're-late people so when we didn't see you last night and you weren't here early, Eve became concerned."

"Yeah, I left before closing. I had dinner with Nova so I kind of prioritized that. I ought to have checked in with you. Sorry."

"We're not your parents," Sheridan said shaking his head. "We were just anxious when you weren't here first thing."

"Especially what with Dr. Ketchall. Did you hear?" Eve asked.

"Yeah. I feel bad for him, and for his family and friends."

"We all feel bad for everybody," Eve said. "Nobody wanted this."

"Somebody did."

"Dave, that's what you're supposed to be unearthing."

"We kept looking for you last night," Eve said with some exasperation. "Not that you could have stopped it, but you might have picked up something that would shed some light on the mystery of his death. You could have told us you were leaving early."

"I'm sorry. I was in and out all day. When I left with Nova I was hoping I wouldn't be coming back so, yes, I ought to have told you."

"That's fine, Dave. We don't need the apology. Just help us out here."

"One thing that'll help me out is if you could tell me who's in our disturbed-aura group. Are the three of us still in it?"

"Sadly, yes," Eve said. "Along with Madame Vadama, Rajiv, the UFOs, and the tantric-sexers. I haven't seen Nova today so hopefully things have lightened up for her, but I doubt it."

"That's too bad, but I'll hold out hope for her. So, what do you know about what happened to Dr. Ketchall? The paper mentioned an unknown substance."

"That's it," Sheridan said. "It could have been anything. Our friends next door swear they tried not to touch him, although they did. Not that I think that killed him, but they do. It guess it might have played a part."

"Wait wait wait. Do we or do we not believe their touch can kill? I thought we'd resolved that."

"We did," Eve said. "But there are turbulent energies here. Systems which contain waves that move with their own rhythm."

"All right," I said, "let's go with the idea that the UFOs contributed in an interstellar way we don't understand. What was it that actually killed him?"

"That's the question. There was no smoking gun, no empty vial, no nothing. Just a body slumped over on his table."

"That's not a good adjustment."

Nor a cure-all for him. But possibly for someone else.

CHAPTER THIRTY

A Good Adjustment

UNLESS DR. KETCHALL HAD chosen to kill himself, he'd died before he'd wanted to. The majority of us die before we want to, and for reasons that are out of our control. Some of those are random, some not. Had the chiropractor died by someone else's hand, as a result of something he'd done, or had some malevolent forces swept him away?

Police tape had been strung up around his booth. Otherwise, things appeared to be the same—if you overlooked the obvious gaps in the bottles and potions that suggested there might have been some pilfering going on. Either that or he'd had big sales right before he died. Did he go out in a blaze of commercial glory? He wouldn't be the first person to worship money and die for it.

While it doesn't make sense to take your own life when you're achieving success, it is a thing. Like the movie or rock star who achieves fame and fortune and realizes that life remains torturous. Most of us believe that life will improve with fame and fortune, and when you attain those things but nothing changes on the inside, you can end up losing hope. So even though it was a long shot that Dr. Ketchall and Gordon, the tantric-sex guy, had done themselves in, I couldn't rule it out.

Still, if truth be told, I wasn't inclined to rule it in either.

I believed I was searching for a killer.

When you're out to catch an animal in the wild, you find its trail and follow it, either forward or backward. Forward, you aim to run across them but could encounter anything. Backward, you might uncover where they sleep and wait there for their return. Backward is the safer option.

I opted to take a tour of the disturbed-aura group and see how everyone was doing. See if there was a trail to follow, preferably one pointing backward.

Nova wasn't in yet. She clearly wasn't a subscriber to my if-you're-not-early-you're-late philosophy. Not a deal breaker. Not an enhancer either, though being with someone who's different than you can balance a relationship. While compromise is an essential part of a relationship, there are times when compromise won't be in your best interests. That said, time could be an issue where compromise was in my best interests, although I'd hold on to a degree of irk.

Rajiv appeared to be in balance; at least, he was smiling as he waved me over.

"Good morning. I need to offer my thanks to you."

"Good morning to you as well. And thank you for the thanks. Anything in particular you're thankful for?"

"You reminded me to be me. I was trying so hard to align myself that I neglected to take the time to let my body rest within itself. That was useful advice, so thank you again."

"You're welcome. Hopefully, business will improve today. I'm sorry that Dr. Ketchall was stricken. That's tough."

"Yes, it is very sad, and he too was out of alignment."

"He was? I didn't notice anything."

"You are not trained as many of us here are. We see things others do not."

"I'm sure of that. What do you think happened to Dr. Ketchall? Did you see anything?"

"I only heard the commotion. I can tell you this, though. He wasn't much of a chiropractor. I spent too much of yesterday watching everybody because business was so slow. His day was worse than mine. Only a few had him do adjustments and not all were pleased."

"A lot of his bottles have been taken, so I assumed business had picked up."

"Scofflaws must have stolen things after the police left. I will tell you what else I observed: All the men trying to impress the Love Doctor. People glancing into your booth and not bothering to stop. The UFO gentlemen being careful not to touch anyone; they too did not have much business. I may need to consider tantric chakra alignment as there was an endless stream checking out the tantric booth. You were over there yourself."

"I did get to do an exercise, which was kind of exciting. I bet if you wrote 'sex' or 'tantric' on your sign, it would garner attention. You've tuned up your sacral chakra. Isn't that the one that has to do with sex? Perhaps you could emphasize that."

"It is a holistic system. Yes, the sacral chakra is related to sexuality, sensuality, and the desire for pleasure. Yet in order to maximize any one chakra, you need to balance them all."

"The tantric-sex angle is drawing the crowds. You'll figure it out."

"Figure what out?" Candy asked.

"Hi," I said.

"A gracious morning to you, Candy," Rajiv said with the kind of enthusiasm only Winnie has for me.

"Good morning to you both. Although I'm afraid with the losses we've had, things are not as good as they might be."

"Yes," said Rajiv, perhaps hoping he might be able to make things as good as they could be for her. "You lost your comrade and the doctor has also been taken. It's upsetting. That's what we were trying to figure out—how you keep your balance when there's such disturbance around you."

"Yes, we've all been affected. It is hard to keep one's balance, but we carry on as best we can."

"There are times," I said, "when I'd prefer to stay in bed all day, but I get myself up and out, and carry on. It's not that hard to go to work when you're feeling fine, but to do it when you feel lousy, well, that's when you're a professional."

"Yes," said Candy. "We're all professionals here."

"You have definitely carried on well. Yesterday you were talking with so many people and signing them up," Rajiv said. "You and your booth are extremely popular."

"People always desire great sex. Tantric takes you into your own essence. It's powerful stuff."

"We are all powerful," Rajiv said. "And I am sure those who have tantric sex with you are treated to a world beyond compare."

"Thank you. And yes, they are, aren't they, Doc?"

"I'd imagine so. From the taste I got, I can confirm there was plenty more to be had."

Rajiv raised his gaze toward the ceiling with a wistful expression. "To be that blessed person."

"Why don't you both drop by at closing time. Let's see what we can do."

"Oh, my goodness," said Rajiv. "I wish we were closing this minute."

I agreed, but not for the same reason.

CHAPTER THIRTY-ONE

The Extraterrestrial Way

TANTRIC SEX WITH Candy would be an experience worth having. Sharing it with Rajiv less so. I was holding out for having my own quasi-tantric experience with Nova. Or at least movement in that direction.

Nova had yet to make an appearance. The UFOs were in attendance but no one was attending to them so I went over.

"Morning, fellas. How you guys doing?"

"It's horrible," One said, more with exasperation than sadness. "We confessed to the police but they wouldn't listen. Neither would Dr. Ketchall. You cannot touch us. Read the sign. We try to avoid contact but they won't listen."

"I'm sorry. It has to be upsetting that death can come to those who touch you if you can't stop them in time."

"But it feels worse," Two said, "when they actually die."

"I'm sure. It's horrible. Can anything reverse it?"

"Certainly," One said. "We know how to fix it."

"That's reassuring."

"Yes and no," Two said. "We know what to do, but we can't do it without help."

One nodded. "Financial help. We can't afford the cure. We've been to hospitals but we don't have the money to pay for their exams."

"Not that we need the exams," Two said.

I tried to lighten things up. "That's sort of how I felt about school back in—"

"We need equipment," One said. "And we're not making enough money here to get it. Everyone is ogling the sex booth."

"Yeah, sex sells. I was just with Rajiv in the chakra-tuning booth where he was lamenting the same thing. Come to think of it, I have an idea for you. Why don't you do an extraterrestrial-sex thing? Something you were exposed to on your journey."

Their faces creased with excitement.

"Well, we did have invasive procedures," Two said.

"There you go. You can modify things. I mean, who's going to say they know better?"

"There are plenty of us, but we only know of a few who've undergone the same invasive procedures."

"Maybe you had sex the alien way. You don't know. Or do you?"

"I don't."

"Me neither."

"What can we do?" Two said. "We can't provide the ultimate orgasm."

"It doesn't have to be the ultimate one—any will do. This will be the extraterrestrial way."

"But we don't know what that is."

"Yes, you do. They taught you and you taught me."

"We did? We don't know the secret."

"Yes, you do. No touching. That's the secret. Be with someone and do the things you want to do, as long as they're okay with it. Just do it without touching."

"We can do that!" they chirped in unison.

CHAPTER THIRTY-TWO

Tantric Fever

TANTRIC FEVER WAS spreading. Eve and Sheridan might adopt the idea as well. I figured I'd pass on bringing it to Nova's attention. Being the Love Doctor was enough; she didn't need to add tantric sex to her moniker. Although that might be worth compromising and slowing down for.

Finally, and fortunately, she showed up. It seemed she was keeping her own hours as it was close to noon. I was itching to touch base with her, but no sooner did she arrive than the line formed.

Since I seemed to be the Pied Piper of tantric sex, I decided to revisit the source—or at least the booth. Unfortunately, Candy wasn't there. Saffron and Phillippe were. Neither were interested in me, no doubt having determined I was not a paying customer, or if I was I was Candy's customer.

During my time in the Navy, I frequented a bar in Subic Bay, Philippines. We were allowed to visit one street in the town—the rest of the city was off limits. So what was on that street that proved such a draw? Bars with bands that played cover songs, and women who'd earn your money. One night, I went to this bar and spent my time and money with a particular woman. Another night, I went back. She wasn't there so I ended up spending time and money with another woman. Then the first woman showed up and made a big stink and called us butterflies.

I learned something in that bar—you pay someone, they have a relationship with you. And they don't want anyone else horning in on it. It's not cricket for someone to take away your customer, nor for the customer to seek another liaison. I'd have been satisfied spending another evening with either woman. After all, I was twenty, I was in the Navy, I was there to see the world while protecting our interests.

Whatever the reason, Saffron and Phillippe's attention was on other interested parties so I hung back and eavesdropped on their conversations. Phillippe, with his dashing looks, fit physique, and wavy slicked-back hair, carried himself like a Grecian god and drew people in like a magnet. Saffron was the go-getter. She reminded me of some of the women I'd seen in that bar in Subic Bay; she put on the charm and acted interested, but her heart and soul were elsewhere. That said, she was sexually alluring, and if I'd been interested in more of what I'd encountered during my Navy years, she wouldn't have been a bad way to go.

They were charging fifteen dollars for ten minutes behind the curtain. There's not a lot you can accomplish tantrically in ten minutes, yet they were lining up. And if the expression on the face of the guy who'd just come through the curtain was anything to go by, the customers were satisfied.

Candy followed him out. She seemed pretty satisfied too. And satisfying. I caught her eye and she came over.

I nodded toward the happy customer. "Whatever you were doing behind that curtain left that guy looking fulfilled."

"There's a lot you can do in ten minutes. You should know that."

"You're right. A short time with you showed me there's a lot I could learn. You must be an excellent teacher."

"That's kind of you to say, but you haven't really seen me in action."

"I've seen enough—you have what it takes."

"And what does it take?" she said as she gave her hair a flick.

"You tell me."

"You gotta have something they want. That's what it takes."

"They're lining up to have sex with you," I said, trying to state an obvious fact and a personal one at the same time.

"That's also kind of you to say, although we're not selling sex. We're sharing the pathway to ecstasy."

"Discovering a pathway to ecstasy is worth more than fifteen dollars."

"The beauty of tantra is that it provides deeper intimacy. It's in service to the other. It's a transcendental approach."

"Which, I guess, is why people are drawn to it."

"Yet others stay away from it because they're afraid."

"They're afraid to have great sex?"

"Sex is powerful. It can overwhelm you. It can be safer to stay away."

I could imagine that sex with Candy could be overwhelming. Sexual desire has led many a person astray. But, as alluring as she was, it might indeed be safer to stay away from her. There were layers to her that were hidden under the sheen.

CHAPTER THIRTY-THREE
Be All You Can Be

Be All You Can Be. It was a recruiting slogan the Army had recently been running. Being a Navy guy, the Army was not where I'd be all that I could be, although I'm not sure I'd been much in the Navy either. I can't speak for others. Being all you can be does have its allure, wherever you do it. It's about realizing your potential and can be exhilarating in that moment.

And yet the pathway to ecstasy isn't a well-traveled road. Giving it all you have to achieve those dreams but not succeeding can hurt. You can console yourself with "At least I tried," but it still sucks. Doesn't matter whether it's exploring having greater sex or pursuing your dream job or asking out a person of interest—there's risk. As a coach in *A Lesson in Baseball and Murder* said, "No risk it, no biscuit."

I moved back into the Garden and hung out with Sheridan and Eve. After ten minutes, it was apparent that they weren't garnering the kind of attention that pays the bills. And Sheridan seemed to be conducting the lion's share of the effort.

Our radio personality entered the booth.

"How's everyone doing?" Dennis said.

Eve gestured to the empty space. "We're okay, but there's hardly any traffic."

"Just wait. Saturday and Sunday, we'll be flooded. You'll see."

"Are you making the rounds?" I asked.

"Just checking how things are going. You have a lovely booth. The traffic will pick up this evening and over the weekend."

"Before you go," Eve said, "do you have any news about the deaths?"

"I'm sorry, I haven't heard anything new. It's horrible what happened but we all need to persist."

"It would be good to get rid of the lookie-loos," Sheridan said. "Could you ask the police to remove the tape and let you have someone take Dr. Ketchall's booth down?"

"I can't do that. Besides, crowds coming over here and checking things out is good for business. You should be welcoming it."

And then he was gone. Eve shook her head.

"I didn't want to tell him but his aura is disturbed too."

I need to come clean regarding Dennis. Yes, he's a famous shrink. Has his own radio call-in show. Gets interviewed by the news media when they need a shrink's perspective. I didn't like his show. I didn't agree with what he said. And having met him, I didn't like him. To his credit, maybe he was being all he could be, even if he did have a disturbed aura.

Perhaps you think I was envious, and I wouldn't deny that. You might say I'd like to have a radio show and tout my own beliefs on the airwaves, and I wouldn't deny that. You might also say I hadn't done all I could do to have a radio show and be a famous shrink, and I wouldn't deny that either.

And you might be thinking that I don't always apply myself as well as I could. I admit to that too.

But just because someone's acquired things I desire doesn't mean they're not also an asshole. I didn't appreciate that he'd told Sheridan he should be welcoming the lookie-loos. Telling others what they should do is a big no-no in the therapy world. It's got its own name: "shoulding." Don't be shoulding on others, or yourself, is what therapists say. Instead, offer suggestions. It was a small thing, but it gave me an additional reason not to like him.

"He's kind of an asshole, isn't he?" I said.

"Dave, he's a promoter. He's full of shit and I definitely don't believe anything he said."

"He's kind of cute," Eve said. "Not cute enough to do more than once but he does have magnetism."

"Cute is in the eye of the beholder," I said.

"He can go fuck himself as far as I'm concerned," Sheridan said.

"Speaking of fucking, I need to share something."

"You got lucky with the Love Doctor last night?"

"I wish. I got 'Let's keep talking.'"

"That's promising," Eve said.

"I hope so. But it's not about that. I've been with some of the neighbors and we've observed the steady stream of customers at the tantric-sex booth."

"Tell me," Eve sighed.

"Rajiv and the UFO guys are changing their signs. Tomorrow they'll be offering tantric extraterrestrial sex and tantric chakra alignment, or the like. You might think about jumping on the bandwagon. We could be a sort of tantric row. It might generate extra business."

"That sounds wonderful, but we don't have anything to do with tantric sex. Not that I'm against it."

"Eve," Sheridan said. "You have plenty to do with tantric sex."

Eve blushed. From what I recalled, their relationship was one of friends with benefits rather than exclusive. It obviously worked for them; they had that ease with each other that's usually associated with coupledom.

"The definitions are loosening up. There are purists out there who'd decry the desecration of the canon. But perhaps you can come up with an angle and exploit it."

"Dave, are you sure you're not a promoter?"

"Yeah, well, I'm certainly not wearing my how-do-you-feel-about-that hat. I'm wearing my trying-to-drum-up-business hat. When I think about therapy, I think about what's therapeutic, what will make things better. I'm simply applying that to the current situation. Getting more customers to buy your potions, lotions, and herbs could make you feel better. And them too."

"Dave, Eve may be a gentle soul, but she's well aware of the bottom line."

"From what I gather, tantra is about accessing the depths and breadths of your being with mantras, meditations, rituals, and yoga. Don't your lotions and potions enhance life?"

"Without a doubt."

"So why not focus on how people can use them with something tantricky?"

"Dave, what are you saying?" Sheridan said. "That we suggest they use the lotions while playing with themselves?"

"You could, although you might begin with the foreplay. Trust me here. Not that I really know what I'm talking about, but you could suggest that they use your lotion/potion while they're doing a deep-breathing, focusing, mantra-ing, yoga-ing thing. Make it a ritual that takes a few minutes… a time to be tantrically connected to themselves."

"Yeah, play with yourself. And what does that do?"

"It makes it—whatever it is—more than it was. Sort of like helping it be all it can be. By giving it focus and extra attention, it makes it special."

Maybe I was getting the hang of this thing after all.

CHAPTER THIRTY-FOUR

Commonalities

TRAFFIC PICKED UP as the afternoon wore on and the aisles and the booths were busier. The array of humanity made for entertaining visuals. Lots of baby boomers questing for life enhancement.

I spent time studying the action in Madame Vadama's booth. She'd escort an interested person behind her curtain; five or ten minutes later, they'd emerge, apparently in possession of a clearer vision of their future. Everyone seemed pleased with what the psychic had told them she'd seen. Other times, she'd sit out front and chat with passersbys. That went on for a while, then the woman I'd seen before returned and stayed for close to forty minutes.

Psychoanalysts see clients four or five times a week. I'm content if I can get someone to come in once a week. Whatever Madame Vadama was doing, she had it going on. When she was finally free, I stepped across the aisle.

"You've been busy."

"Yes, troubling times bring out the hordes. They hunger to know what the future brings."

"It must be a blessing and curse to have that skill."

"It is never a curse to know the truth."

"Yeah, curse is too strong a word. Let's call it a heavy responsibility."

"The truth is never heavy. It is light. A beacon."

"A beckoning beacon. I never thought about it that way. When I come upon a truth it does provide a path. Though some truths are more pleasant than others, they do guide the way. I have a question. I've noticed that you go behind the curtain for five or ten minutes, but there's one woman who stays longer."

"She's one of my regulars."

"It helps to have regulars. She's familiar but I can't place her."

"I can't tell you who she is. Like you, I honor my customers' privacy."

I often run into professional integrity when I don't expect it. It's not that I don't have my own, although mine tends to be looser around the edges. And while I hadn't expected Madame Vadama to tell me that her regular was an actress and I'd probably seen her in a movie, I had hoped she'd give me a clue. But like a lot of things in life, it was clear that if I wanted to know more I'd have to do more.

"As well you should," I said. "If she comes back I might have to ask her if she recognizes me. My memory is not the best."

"Let me ask you something. If you had a client who was in a marriage where she was undervalued and not fully appreciated, what would you tell her to do?"

"I'd ask her what she felt, thought, and wanted to do."

"Yes, I'm sure. But what would you tell her to do?"

"I'd tell her I was sorry and it couldn't be easy. I'd ask her if she'd told her partner how she felt. And if she had, I'd ask her how that had gone."

"Yes, that's a positive thing she could do, and you'd be showing plenty of empathy. But what would you tell her to do?"

"I'd throw in strategies and techniques to assist her in getting more of what she wants, things that would support her through the process."

"That's nice. But what would you tell her, looking ahead to the future?"

"Isn't that your job?"

"Yes, but come on. What would you tell her?"

"I'd tell her what you and I quite likely tell everybody: that I saw things resolving themselves and her being happier down the road."

Madame Vadama smiled. "Our jobs have quite a lot in common, after all."

CHAPTER THIRTY-FIVE
Zanzibar

EVE AND SHERIDAN left me in charge while they went for dinner. On the way out of the booth, Eve told me Nova's aura remained disturbed. I had mixed feelings. On the one hand, I wasn't pleased with the idea she was still psychically in poor shape, but on the other I was glad she was still in the group.

With no dinner plans, I was left with no other option but to observe the steady stream of people lining up for the Love Doctor. I have voyeuristic tendencies and enjoy watching and overhearing conversations. The person who cuts my hair told me she calls it salon ears. As a therapist, I might get away with calling it fieldwork, but honestly, I have salon ears.

People told Nova their love problems, and asked her how to fix them. The first five minutes were free, but after that the meter switched on. The majority of her customers got out after five minutes, although one guy was there for over fifteen.

Eavesdropping can be frustrating; the narrative thread isn't necessarily easy to pick up. I heard words that I'd heard before—"real estate" and "malpractice"—but couldn't make any sense of them without the context.

Eve's Garden still wasn't drawing them in. Either we didn't have

CHAPTER THIRTY-NINE
Touching Base

I HAD A couple of things to do before the expo closed at nine: First and foremost, get a next step with Nova. If I bumped into a dead end, well, there was the option of joining Rajiv and seeing where that led. More likely I'd go home and sulk with Winnie and have her share her non-judgmental dog love.

I went back to the booth, sat upfront, and eavesdropped on Nova. I'd make my move as soon as there was a lull. The procession coming down the aisle caught me off guard. Bennett, Louise, and Lucky. Bennett stopped off at the tantric-sex booth. Louise and Lucky left him to it. While there might be moves Louise could learn, I doubted that long, drawn-out sex would be good for business. I also doubted the tantric pace would sync well with the cocaine sprinting through Bennett's bloodstream.

"Hey, Doc," said Louise, giving me one of her all-encompassing hugs. "How are you holding up?"

"I'm holding my own. How are you two?"

"Bennie's been getting restless, so we decided we'd check in with you. You always manage to calm him."

"Thanks, but calming Bennett—no one can master that. I'm glad you think my efforts help. I know yours do, too."

"It's like getting the rooster to go back to sleep once he's seen the light," Lucky said.

"I'm sure," I said. "And it looks like he might be trying out some tantric sex later."

"No, he won't," said Louise with an assuredness I rarely have. "Our boy doesn't have the patience for that. He's trying to recruit add-ons for the night."

"Those tantric people could be candidates. They're kind of off from the rest of the crowd here. Go take a closer look at them. If they weren't here I'd say they'd worked for you in Vegas."

"It's a growing profession. Branching out and incorporating. Sex sells. Just got to discover how to package it. It's all in the packaging."

"Which is why you're so successful. Well, that and the brains to go with the package."

"Thanks, Doc, but you need to help Bennett out with Mr. Russo and Caddy or he's going to blow it all."

"There may be an upside to that, but he's not ready to trim things back yet; he still wants to push the boundaries. That's great and yet it does increase the odds of having a rough time with the comeuppance."

"It's the blustering, complaining, whining, and kvetching that will be hard to deal with," Lucky said. "He doesn't need the money, but he doesn't want to lose it."

"I agree. He won't be pleasant to be around if things go south. I have the slightest hint of the essence of a way forward for him, but I need you two to keep him reined in for a while longer."

"That's promising," Louise said. "But, it's always touch and go with him."

"Yeah. Let's touch base tomorrow. If you need me, we've got each other's beeper numbers. Louise, why don't you go join Bennett and see what's holding his attention while I have a quick chat with Lucky?"

"I'll see you boys later. Don't get into too much mischief…" She smirked and sashayed off.

I watched her sway away and turned to Lucky. "How are things really going with Bennett? Do we need to worry more than usual?"

"Louise is keeping him in check, but he's like that pony in my cousin Ivo's backyard. When he gets a chance he's gonna try to jump the fence. Then the neighbors will be complaining."

"Yeah, he's prone to being a loose cannon, and he aspires to be even looser. I suspect he's hoping that the reviewers of his movie will write that he's outrageous. That'll please him."

"Sooner or later he's gonna blow it unless we find a way to help him out."

"Speaking of which, if you can leave him safely for a moment or two, and take a stroll through the aisles, I think something might catch your attention."

"The doctor next door is getting plenty of attention but I knew you wouldn't appreciate my infringing. Besides, I've got my eye on the brunette over there in the shiatsu-massage booth."

"I can definitely see the upside there. While you're sparking, keep an eye out. See what else you can see."

CHAPTER FORTY
Oomphy

"Who are your friends?"

"Nova, I didn't see you there. I'd have been happy to introduce you."

"That's all right. I've met plenty of folks today. I'm about to leave. I'll see you in the morning."

"How about I escort you to your car?"

"Let's go."

I enjoyed watching her walk. She had a long stride and carried herself with the kind of assurance that complemented her looks. We got to her Mustang and she leaned her back against it, facing me. I considered going for the kiss, but held back.

"How about having breakfast together? Zucky's opens early."

"That's where you want to take me?"

"Impressive, huh? Some say it's the best deli in town. Others say top three. Hard to beat that."

"You really do know how to impress a girl."

"I like to think so, but not act so."

"You want to appear humbler than you are."

"For a while at least. I'm plenty aware there are things I don't do well and others I do relatively well, so I don't get overly taken away with myself."

"But you are taken?"

"Well, yeah. Guilty as charged. But, come on, if you're not taken with you, who else will be? You have to play the hand you're dealt and do your best to be all you can be."

"Are you being the best you can be right now?"

"I'm feeling pretty oomphy."

"Oomphy?"

"Yeah. I'm pretty oomphy. How about you? You feeling oomphy?"

"That wouldn't be my word. Though it fits."

"What would be your word?"

"Intrigued would cover it."

"I like that. I'm intrigued too. Intrigue is everywhere. Why not feel it?"

"With that, it's time for me to say goodnight."

We agreed to meet at Zucky's at eight thirty.

I thought again about going in for that first kiss. Or asking if she was up for giving it a try. But I wasn't getting any indicators that either would be welcome. Instead, I tried to be content with her being intrigued. Better than giving her reason not to be.

CHAPTER FORTY-ONE

What's Money For?

I WAS MAKING headway with Nova. Not at the pace I'd have preferred, but at a pace that was probably preferable. I was excited, though whiney too.

I don't want you to get the wrong impression. I have a healthy interest in having a healthy sex life with someone other than myself. Since puberty that's been high on my list of life's priorities. There are times I've been more interested in the sex than the relationship, but as I've gotten older, sex for sex's sake has lost much of its appeal. I'm not saying under the right circumstances I wouldn't do it. I'm just saying I don't seek it out. These days, I'm hoping for a life partner with whom I can have a healthy sex and love life.

I considered the invitation to join Rajiv and discover what Candy had in mind. Tantric or otherwise, I wasn't interested in a threesome with them. Nor did time alone with Candy, with Rajiv in line before or after, hold any allure. Truthfully, Candy was someone I'd prefer to take home and have sex with in my fantasies rather than in reality.

I couldn't deny my curiosity though. I hadn't discerned what the tantric-sexers were about, but something was off with them. I'd had my free sample but I hadn't put any time or money into the pot to learn more. I might need to go behind the curtain.

I watched the yellow Mustang drive out of the parking lot and returned inside and headed directly to the chakra-tuning booth.

"What do you think she wants to do?" Rajiv asked.

"I'm guessing she wants to fuck you. Me too. Or something else entirely. I'm not interested in fucking her. I'm supportive of your doing that... if that's what you want."

"You bet it is. I'm not delusional. She isn't inviting me because she's attracted to me. I'm some after-hours extra money for her. But it is after hours, and if she chose me, why not? What's money for if not to buy you pleasure?"

We both turned toward the tantric-sex booth. Saffron, Phillippe, and Candy were closing down. As soon as Candy was on her own, Rajiv headed over. I followed behind. He had that awkward gait of someone who's trying to be cool but isn't. If Candy was put off by such awkwardness, she didn't show it. Instead, she greeted Rajiv with a nice long hug. Then I got one. She knew how to move into you, fill the spaces, and arouse you. Maybe I'd do that threesome after all.

"Boys, how are you? Are you ready to go have a good time?"

"Am I ready? You kidding? Let's do it," Rajiv said.

"What about you?"

"I'll leave the good time to you two."

"You don't know what you're missing."

"That's why I can walk away. If you told me, I'd want to come."

"It will be more sex than you've ever had in your life. And more arousing. It will take you places you've only beaten off to. If you boys are ready, the ship is getting underway."

Rajiv was close to hyperventilating. "I'm all in."

"You two have a memorable night. Rajiv, you can tell me all about it tomorrow, if you show up."

Oh no. Had I cursed him? I did hope he wouldn't show up, but only because he was still going at it or because he was sleeping blissfully, not because he'd flopped over somewhere, the lifeblood oozing from his chakras.

CHAPTER FORTY-TWO

Moving

Saturday, August 10, 1985

I SKIPPED MY oatmeal with banana and blueberries and just read the *LA Times*. The riots were getting worse in South Africa, the Food and Drug Administration was banning preservatives that were killing us, Barry Goldwater had said the super-secret stealth bomber was shaped like a wing, the Dodgers had lost, and the Woo-Woo Death Expo had made the front page of the California section.

The cause of death for both victims was unknown. The UFO guys' poisonous touch had gotten noted. And while the paper hadn't made light of the killings, they had spent an inordinate amount of time on the UFO angle. Plus, an astrologer had explained how Mercury was in retrograde, meaning bad things were liable to happen.

Regardless of what Mercury was doing, things didn't feel right. I suspected Dennis of lying about the booth allocations. And the tantric-sex crew were off-kilter. It was like they'd broken in one day, killed off all the real tantric practitioners, and replaced them. Perhaps they really were aliens of one kind or another.

According to Eve, I was feeling precisely what I was supposed yet even to get to first base and kiss her. She might opt out at any time. And there I was already worrying whether I was taking on more than I could handle. I needed to stay in the moment and let things evolve, but at the same time I was planning what would happen a year from now.

I arrived back at the expo, relieved at least to see that Rajiv had made it through the night. He looked drained but invigorated. I made a note to ask him if his chakras had gotten realigned and to ask Eve if his aura had shifted. If either were the case, perhaps we all needed to book time with Candy.

In the meantime, Sheridan was beckoning me into Eve's Garden.

"Here, give me a hand," he said as he lifted one end of their new sign. It read: *Eve's Tantric Garden.*

"This ought to get some attention," I said. "Have you and Eve worked up a sales pitch you'd like to fill me in on?"

"We have, Dave. Eve has created the tantric elixir—a unique medley of herbs and potions that will release the toxins that block your full destiny. Your body will be taken to a primal blissful state. Truly cleansed, you will radiate and receive the purest gift of life."

"I'll take it. What is the purest gift of life?"

"Dave, that will only come to light when you use the elixir. Keep the mystery. Ten dollars a jar usually. But, lucky you, we're having an expo special—two for fifteen."

"Customers like deals."

"You're welcome to go off script as we haven't really refined it."

"So, basically, when you take a bath with the herbs, you feel clean, which does make me feel better if I'm going to be rubbing up against someone else."

"Dave, let's not make this about your taking a bath and your sex life. The emphasis needs to be on the release of toxins and the deeper cleansing that frees your cells."

"Is there a shower version? I'm not a bath guy."

"Soak a sponge in the herbs first."

"Will that make any difference?"

"Dave, the thing here is to relax. The shower won't do that; it's more invigorating. But if they think it will cleanse them, it will. Remember? You taught me that."

"I probably said that if you believe something to be true, it will be true for you, even if it isn't."

"There you go. Welcome to Eve's Tantric Garden."

was if she had to stop for a light. Unless she was running it. Which she did with a frequency that was alarming.

This is when the job gets tricky. I was following her for no reason I could explain to a cop if they pulled me over. It was one thing to speed along San Vicente Boulevard, but something else to run the light at Twenty-Sixth Street where the Brentwood Country Mart was located. Plenty of police cars were parked there while the cops loaded up on barbeque chicken and fries.

I don't enjoy breaking laws. I don't mind bending them, though what I consider bending you might consider breaking. But running a red light at a major intersection? That could give anyone bad luck for the day or more.

I made it through without seeing any flashing red lights in my rearview mirror, which made me wonder if not getting caught had been the bad luck. It's hard to tell sometimes.

The psychic took a left onto La Mesa Drive. Behind the houses on the right stood the Riviera Country Club. Occasionally, I'd glimpse the greenery and the large Spanish-style clubhouse. This was a neighborhood I could drive through but not afford to live in. After a quarter mile or so, she stopped in front of a massive modern not-my-style house and hurried in.

I drove on past. There was close to no traffic on the street and few parked cars. I made a U-turn and parked next to a gardener's truck.

I didn't want to be there long. If it had been nighttime I'd have listened to Fernando Venezuela pitch. But it was late morning so I settled in for the short haul, figuring I'd stay until I got too hungry, too in need of a bathroom, or too much attention from a neighbor.

After an hour, Madame Vadama came out along with the woman I recognized but still couldn't place. The woman appeared agitated. Perhaps my advice to the madame hadn't been useful. The woman returned inside and Madame Vadama drove off. I had a decision to make: follow the Beamer or wait a little longer because the mail delivery truck was making its rounds down the street. While I can lean toward action, I'm also fine with inaction. I waited.

As the mail carrier finished delivering the mail I had a talk with myself. I'd run a red light earlier. While not desirable, it doesn't typically get you in a whole lot of trouble. Opening someone's mailbox, however, is a different ball game. It probably won't get you thrown in jail but it does fall into the category of a federal offense. Being locally minded, I tend to avoid federal offenses.

So I wrote a note—*Sorry I missed you. See you soon.* I scribbled an indecipherable version of my name at the bottom and pretended I was leaving it in the box. That's when I stole a peek.

Mr. and Mrs. Albert Russo.

I knew that name. I knew that woman. Now I'd to put them together.

CHAPTER FORTY-NINE
Why Me?

IT WAS MID-AFTERNOON and I was thinking of Winnie. One of my neighbors holds herself as Winnie's other parent and when I'm out of town or have long days, she walks and feeds her. Today, however, she hadn't been available. I have a dog door so Winnie can go into the backyard—which also means the possums can come in—so I had figured that she'd hold out till I got home. But with the inner lives of dogs on my mind, I was motivated to go home early, play with her, take her on a walk, and give her an early dinner.

I live on the wrong side of the mountains that cut across LA. Back in the day, when I lived with my parents on the right side, I'd make fun of those who lived in the valley. The movie *Valley Girl* had come out a couple of years ago and showed the world the exaggerated materialistic simple-mindedness of the local residents. That had encouraged others to throw in a *like* in the middle of sentence and a *whatever* at the end to valley up their dialogue.

My home has a degree of privacy and from what language of Winnie's I can understand, she's content with it. We played a bit on the floor and had a pleasant walk. She devoured her kibble almost as fast as I poured it. And I brushed my teeth and combed my hair in case things picked up with Nova.

Winnie stared at me as I left, and I had one of those heart-tugging moments. Her eyes were saying, *Why are you leaving your best friend alone in the house?* Ugh. My aura didn't feel too bright as I slinked out in a haze of guilt.

The street I live on wiggles its way up the mountain only so far. To get back to the wealthier side of town I needed to go back down the lesser side of the mountain and onto the freeway.

There's not a lot of traffic on my dead-end road, and a number of side streets that branch off down to the valley floor. I mention this because if I were to follow someone on my street, I'd have to stay close behind them.

I don't usually spend much time checking my rearview mirror because it's hard to go over the speed limit. But maybe Winnie had seen into the future and psychically told me to keep an eye out.

Because someone was following me.

Could be a neighbor. That was a possibility. But I was in sleuthing mode so I was warier than usual.

The popular direct turn-off to the freeway was coming up. I continued past it. So did they. Not entirely unusual. But not usual either.

If they were following me, what would I do? Try to lose them? Or try not to lose them and get a peek when I could?

The bad news was they knew where I lived. That made trying to lose them penny wise and pound foolish. They kept sufficient distance between us that I couldn't discern if it was a man or woman in the driver's seat. What I could tell was that it was a black Chevy Camaro.

They tailed me all the way back to the Santa Monica Civic. I have to admit, it kind of freaked me out. I've followed suspects—heck, I'd followed Candy and Madame Vadama—but I'd never been followed. At least, not to my knowledge.

By the time I arrived at the booth I was ready to ask Eve for calming lotions, Rajiv for chakra tuning, Madame Vadama for a check-in on my future, and Nova for any form of comfort she was willing to extend.

CHAPTER FIFTY

Had Been

"Dave, you need to apologize to Eve."

"What did I do?"

"It's nothing you've done recently. Eve's not a big reader, yet when she heard you'd written a book about the US Festival and our time together there, she was eager to read it. She won't tell you, but I know she was upset with what you wrote about her."

"I'm sorry to hear that. I tried to represent everyone fairly."

"And for the most part you did that, but that doesn't mean people will necessarily like reading your fair description of themselves."

"Yeah, things can be a bit harsher in black and white. Anything in particular get under her skin? I can try to balance things out."

"It's too late. You wrote that she was a bridesmaid and never a bride, and that hit a raw nerve."

"I can see how it might. Anything else?"

"That was the worst. That and observing how hard living had taken its toll on her."

"As I recall, I also said she'd been a beauty."

"Perhaps you can appreciate how the past-perfect might have rankled."

"I get that. If I write a book about this I'll make sure to include how much better she looked since I'd last seen her."

"That would be wise. Listen, Dave, maybe one of these years, Eve and I will settle down, but don't count on it. If you could find your way to helping her get involved with someone, then she won't be a bridesmaid because he'll either make her a bride or I'll get jealous enough to take the plunge and do it myself."

So now I needed to make things good with Eve on top of everything else. I've never considered myself a matchmaker, although at my twentieth high-school reunion a few months earlier I'd managed to get my one surfing buddy connected with the prettiest woman in our class.

I was mulling over my liaising skills when Lucky swung by.

"Hey, Doc. How you doing?"

"I'm holding up. Did you come by yourself or do you have company?"

"I'm checking things out before they get here. Bennett wants to have his palm read and Louise wants to check out Quantum Health and the Dream Café. I hope you got something brewing because Rip's here. He must also be casing the joint, hoping they'll show up so he can tail them."

"That might be. But I have a sense that he's following me."

"You? You said he was kind of a fan, but why would he be following you?"

"Your guess is as good as mine. It might not be him, but someone followed me here not long ago."

"Isn't that a late arrival for you?"

"It would be but I was here earlier. I drove home to feed and walk the dog. I spotted someone tailing me when I left the house. A black Chevy Camaro. No idea how long they've been on my trail."

"Why would someone follow you? You sure you're not being paranoid?"

"Unless one of neighbors left their house the same time I did and took the long way here, we can assume they're following me."

"Nothing personal, Doc, but who'd be interested in you? Don't tell me it's the Love Doctor. Is it? Did she follow you?"

"Let's not talk about my fantasy life. She threw me a curveball this morning and I'm digesting it. She told me she's going to leave LA within a year to move to Santa Fe."

"Didn't you once tell me to follow my heart?"

"Yeah, I might have, but that doesn't mean I would. Plus, I'm not confident I'm in love with her yet. I'd prefer to hold off on that until I at least kiss her. And she might want to weigh in herself. I don't think I could move to Santa Fe. That would have to be the kind of love I've never experienced before."

"You also told me that love is about expanding and enhancing. If that materialized, she might be worth the move."

"It does sound reasonable. Yet do I invest a year with her only to have her go her own way? If I loved her that much, and she could deal with me, I'd have to move to a place I have no desire to go and where there's no one I know. Tough call."

"Maybe it'll be easier once you get that kiss. You don't have to decide all that right now."

"You're right. I can wait a day. But I do like to get to the end before I get to the beginning."

"It can be helpful to get thrown a curveball," Lucky said. "It ups your focus."

He'd been thrown his own curveball not long ago and was grateful for it. Maybe I would be too.

"Yeah. That's true. It also reminds me that other curveballs might be thrown at me down the line."

"Doc, don't worry about the future. You got other things to fret about."

"I do?"

"Yeah, you do," he said. He waved at someone and beckoned them over.

"Lucky and Doc. I'm so happy to see you both," Rip said, shaking Lucky's hand and hugging me.

"Rip, it's a pleasure to see you as well. Did you hear that Doc was here and come to see what he was selling?"

"No. Not that I wouldn't come to see you but I'm otherwise employed. We just bumped into each other."

"It's a small town," I said.

Rip looked away from us. "I don't mean to be rude, but I can't stand here. I'm leaving. And Doc, if you're free would you meet me at the end of the aisle?"

Rip hurried away and Lucky said, "What does that mean?"

"I'll tell you what it means. It means Rip might not be following me. I bet Madame Vadama is behind those curtains over there, talking to a woman I recognized but couldn't identify, but now can."

"My Uncle Vlado once ran into this woman. He goes up to her and tells her she looks familiar. And you won't believe what she says? She says, 'We were married once.' Uncle Vlado ain't the sharpest tack."

"I can relate. I'm pretty sure Rip's following her, and me, and maybe our pals, which doesn't sound possible. I'll touch base with Rip, see what he wants. Can you keep an eye on things here? I imagine Rip will be glancing this way as well."

Lucky nodded and we parted ways.

CHAPTER FIFTY-ONE

Beck and Call

I WENT TO the end of the aisle but couldn't see Rip. Either he was better at hide and seek than me, or other matters had taken precedence. I went back and hung out with Lucky.

"Standing here watching Madame Vadama's booth has got me nostalgic for my Aunt Selveta. She spoke with the spirits too."

"How did those conversations go?"

"Someone would ask her what a dearly departed had to say to them and she'd tell them."

"It'd be hard to argue it wasn't true, but do you think she was genuine?"

"Yes and no. I'll tell you why she was trusted—she could see into people's heads. She could tell what they were thinking, even if they weren't thinking it. Like you shrinks do. She saw what they wanted so that's what she told them she'd heard."

"I suppose it's possible to hear what the dead are saying in an indirect way. I often ask clients to 'talk' with someone they're no longer in contact with, and they're able to create a conversation. It's kinda the same thing. We can all have a sense of what they might say."

"Like you, Aunt Selveta had empathy. It lets you see into others."

"You have to come with me."

A hand grabbed mine and I turned. Bennett.

"Let's go," he said, and pulled.

"Can we do it later? We're kind of on a stakeout here."

"Lucky can stay. You gotta come."

"Hold on. Lucky, just keep an eye out and you can fill me in later. Or Aunt Selveta can tell me. Hopefully, I won't be gone long."

Being on call is one thing. Being at someone's beck and call is another. I don't want to be the guy who's told to jump and asks, "How high?" It bothered me that Bennett might think of me that way. The guy was used to getting his way. And I was used to charging him for it. I needed to remember that.

"Louise demanded I take preventative medicine," he said as we approached her at the end of the aisle, in front of the primal-scream booth.

"What are we trying to prevent?"

"The usual," Louise said, giving me the kind of hug that leaves an impression. "Bennie is getting hard to handle. I'm down with getting hookers involved, and if we were in Vegas I'd take care of it. But it's too risky here. Mr. Russo and Caddy got connections; it's not worth it. But that's me talking. Bennie, you explain to the doc what you want."

"Yes, my goddess. I want to take it to the limit. Louise is the limit and she knows I know it. And she also knows that when we add in talent, it takes a great thing and makes it stratospheric. I don't care about the money. Well, of course I care. Have you gotten the goods yet on those bastards? You gotta get them off my back. I can't hold out much longer."

"I'm glad to know you can hold out longer. That's important. You keep holding out. And if you can't, well, go to Vegas. It's only a short flight."

"That's what I told him too," Louise said, "but he has to meet with them tomorrow. They have some scenes they want to cut. That isn't going to go well. We may need you there."

"So wait. You have a meeting tomorrow. Can't you at least hold out till then?"

"It's iffy. The tension makes me act out."

"I get that. Why don't you and Louise have an erotic tour of LA? Go do strange things in strange locations. Just keep the coke well-hidden because you can take it as a given that Rip will be watching."

"That turns me on. I don't like hiding, but it's erotic. We can do that. But you gotta be at the meeting tomorrow."

"Where and when?"

"Mr. Russo's house in Santa Monica. Ten a.m."

Beck and call it was.

CHAPTER FIFTY-TWO
Broken Record

WE ALL MULTI-TASK whether we like it or not. My weekend assignment had been to be an ounce of prevention for the forces Eve felt would be causing a disturbance. So far I hadn't prevented anything. Nor did I have a clue how to stem the tide. I was in danger of not fulfilling my job assignment.

Or part of it, because then Bennett had descended. Not only had I been tasked with getting Mr. Russo and Caddy off his back; I now also had to facilitate a meeting with them at Mr. Russo's house. That would make me late to the expo. I talked myself around that by rationalizing that I wasn't exactly doing the nine to five.

Odds were that Bennett would be wired and outraged and the producers would be calm and in control. During our previous meeting, Bennett had sat between the two of them, taken out a vial of cocaine, and snorted up a couple of times before inviting them to join in. They'd declined. A move like that tomorrow wouldn't go down well. Not that it had before. But now, it might just tip him out of favor.

I chose to deal with tomorrow tomorrow. *Funny*, I thought. I had no difficulty putting off dealing with his issue until I needed to deal with it, yet I wanted to make decisions now based on how I'd feel about Nova in a year's time. That is, if there was still a mutual interest in finding out.

Lucky was gone, Candy and Phillippe were carrying larger loads, the UFOs were selling secrets, Eve and Sheridan's gardening seemed to be paying off, Rajiv was in balance, Nova was gone, and Madame Vadama waved me over.

"Hello," I said. "Nice to have a bit of respite."

"None of us are here for respite."

"I hope we haven't run into any of that bad luck you saw in the cards."

"One never fully knows. I need to ask you something. You told me that if you were counseling someone who was undervalued you'd give them strategies and techniques to get more of what they want. Are you willing to share those with me?"

"There's no slam dunk that's a hundred percent effective. It often depends on how you do something rather than what you do."

"Yes, but come on."

"My favorite technique is called the broken record. Like a record that gets stuck and repeats the same thing over and over?"

"That sounds like you."

"I'm certainly a practitioner, but the technique has a bit more going for it. You buy something in a store, realize you made a mistake, and ask for a refund. The store tells you it's too late to return it. You tell them you understand and want your money back. They tell you they're sorry but the policy clearly states no returns. You tell them you agree with the policy, it's a fair one, that if it were your store you'd have the same one, and you want your money back. You keep understanding their point of view and re-affirming yours."

"That's fine in the store, but what about real life?"

"Tell her to be understanding, to agree with her partner's point of view, and—not but—*and* she wants what she wants."

"And that will…"

"Increase the number of times she gets what she wants. It gives her a way to stand up for herself while being sensitive to his needs. In those kinds of confrontational moments, it's reassuring to have a bit of a script to guide you through. She won't get what she wants all the time, and sometimes she'll have to back down, but she'll see improvement."

Madame Vadama nodded, waved her hand in the air, and said, "Poof."

CHAPTER FIFTY-THREE

Heart to Heart

I'VE ACKNOWLEDGED THAT I'm not a good learner and I'd just demonstrated it to myself. Again. Madame Vadama had asked me for something, but I hadn't asked her for anything in return.

The police had cordoned off a portion of the tantric-sex booth so Candy and Phillippe were still able to ply their trade. They were busier than usual so the chances of my speaking alone with either one were remote.

"Do we have a volunteer?" Candy said looking directly at me.

While volunteering can bring rewards, more often than not it's the opposite. Or maybe that was just Navy life when they picked the volunteers.

"Thank you," Candy said. She took my hand and led me toward a mat on the floor.

"I'm so sorry to hear about Saffron."

"Thanks. But we don't have time to chat right now."

"Candy and this gentleman will demonstrate a simple yet powerful position you can easily try at home," Phillippe said. "While they're preparing, let me give you all a brochure containing lots of valuable information."

Candy whispered in my ear, "I have to speak with you. Meet me tonight when things close up. It's very important."

She sat cross-legged and had me do the same. Our knees almost touched. Phillippe instructed us to put our right hand on the other's heart chakra, and our left hand on top of the other's right.

"Attend to your heart. Feel it within your chest, then tune in to the energy and emotion that fill and surround it."

I'd have been uncomfortable enough doing this in my living room with Candy, but with a dozen onlookers, I was having trouble getting out of my head and into my heart.

"How is your heart? Can you feel its beat?"

I tried to breathe and look deeply into her eyes. It made me light-headed.

"Bring your breathing into union."

I was getting high. Not sexy, more woozy, and I felt incredibly close to Candy. I was lost in time and place. When Phillippe called an end to our exercise I was ready for a nap.

Or maybe a roll in the hay with Candy.

CHAPTER FIFTY-FOUR

Appreciation

IT WAS CLOSE to dinner time and I was still a little loopy. I didn't truly have a desire to roll in the hay with Candy. It was just the afterglow of the tantric-sex thing. In reality, I'd felt a soul connection with her—two people trying to make their way in the world. Fellow travelers.

The person I wanted/wasn't sure I wanted to travel with was busy. I hung out at the corner of Eve's Tantric Garden, waiting for a quiet moment to connect with Nova.

"Sheridan told me to be nicer to you."

"Really, Eve? You've been more than nice. You've been pleasant company. I've enjoyed spending this time with you."

"That's nice, but he told me I need to appreciate you for who you are and who you're not."

"That can be hard to do."

"I do appreciate your trying to help us out even if you haven't been much help. You're trying and that counts for something."

"Thanks. I do like to be appreciated, yet it's not often present in the quantity I crave."

"You're not alone," Sheridan said.

"I have unrealistic expectations."

"Most assuredly, but even those with realistic ones come up short."

"I was in Vegas once and took acid with friends. We had our own fear-and-loathing weekend, and at one point I ended up playing a slot machine and lamenting that it wouldn't reward me because I was a nice fellow. It seemed so unfair."

"There's no reward for being nice, Dave."

Eve nodded. "And you don't need to drop acid to know that life's unfair."

Well, now there's one parked down the block from me. That's too much of a coincidence. If you can get over here, perhaps you can park nearby and see how the driver spends the evening."

CHAPTER FIFTY-EIGHT

Raymond Chandler, Dashiell Hammett, John O'Hara, Dorothy Parker, F. Scott Fitzgerald, Charlie Chaplin, W.C. Fields, Jean Harlow, Marlene Dietrich, Greta Garbo, Rudolph Valentino, Orson Welles, Marilyn Monroe, and Humphrey Bogart, to Name a Few

THREE DOORS. WHICH one would Madame Vadama pick? Follow Phillippe? Wait and see if Mr. Russo and Caddy came out? Or haul ass back to the Civic in time to get into the socially acceptable dinner-time window?

Madame Vadama would follow her intuition, so that's where I started. The odds were Phillippe would go back to the Civic, so when he strolled out to his car I watched him drive away. There was an alleyway at the end of the building. Soon, a white Cadillac convertible came out. Even if the top hadn't been down I'd have spotted that it was carrying Mr. Russo and Caddy.

I followed them, hoping Lucky was following whoever was following me, and said goodbye to dinner with Nova and after-dinner with Nova. If I got lucky, I'd get back to the Civic before she left and could grovel at her feet while I explained my tardiness. She was probably used to groveling. My standing her up might even earn me some points once she understood why. Wishful thinking? I hoped not.

Caddy and Mr. Russo drove west on Hollywood Boulevard for five minutes, took a right, and entered a parking lot. I held back for a moment at the corner, then turned right and drove past the lot. They got out of their car and went into Musso & Frank Grill.

I've never eaten there. Plenty have, among them Raymond Chandler, Dashiell Hammett, John O'Hara, Dorothy Parker, F. Scott Fitzgerald, Charlie Chaplin, W.C. Fields, Jean Harlow, Marlene Dietrich, Greta Garbo, Rudolph Valentino, Orson Welles, Marilyn Monroe, and Humphrey Bogart, to name a few. Someday I'll make the pilgrimage. At the moment, I was parked down the street and getting hungry.

By the time they'd finished dinner and I'd followed them to their next destination, the expo would be closed for the night and I'd need to go home, walk Winnie, and have her commiserate with me.

I'm a fast eater, but when I go to a restaurant with tablecloths, I don't usually finish in half an hour. Not so them. They were back in the car in under thirty minutes. Caddy made his way over to Sunset and headed west. It was Saturday evening and the strip was getting busy. Hollywood Boulevard and this portion of Sunset are on every tourist's list of places to go. I don't cruise it anymore but it's good for people-watching, which makes up for the traffic. Even I know that sometimes you have to slow down and enjoy the view.

That, however, was not what Caddy had in mind. He changed lanes frequently, honked the horn at dawdling tourists, and made it back to Mr. Russo's pad in Santa Monica in record time.

Whatever Caddy did next, he'd do with a tail: me. Or two: the black Chevy. Or three: Lucky.

CHAPTER FIFTY-NINE

One Too Many Maybes

CADDY WENT SOUTH.

My mind was buzzing—data coming at me from all directions. I tried to keep the threads tied but they kept branching out. Going to Mr. Russo's house on La Mesa Drive, the one Madame Vadama had been to, confirmed that the woman I'd recognized but couldn't place was Mrs. Russo.

I'd never met her but I remembered her now. In *A Lesson in Comedy and Murder* I sort of broke into the house Mr. Russo was staying in and saw a framed photograph of her with her husband.

She must be Madame Vadama's undervalued, under-appreciated client whose husband had gone out for a drink with his partner before coming home. Had Mr. Russo assigned Rip to keep an eye on her? He wouldn't be the first rich older guy to have his young wife followed.

I'd assumed Mr. Russo was having Rip follow Bennett to catch him doing coke so he could enforce the morality clause in their contract. I'd also assumed Rip was following me.

Rip ought to ask for a raise.

The longer Caddy drove, the less vigilant I became. Soon, we were back at the Civic parking lot.

I'm big on hope. It picks your spirits up. Mine were certainly up, primarily because there was a chance I'd be able to grovel to Nova. Yet I was also curious about why Caddy was here. Was he meeting up with Phillippe and heading out to Malibu for some group sex?

I followed him into the expo. He paid his admission and walked in like a tourist at Disneyland. I couldn't believe that flickering candles, burning incense, and New Age music would be how he set the mood in his home, nor how he chose to spend his Saturday nights out of it, and yet he didn't appear the least taken aback.

He marched down aisles until he found Phillippe. They exchanged serious words and then he left.

I'd hoped to see Nova, having rehearsed my apology/excuse speech a few hundred times, but she was nowhere to be seen. It was likely the case that she'd called it a night after being stood up for the second time.

I followed Caddy back out into the night. We ended up over at his house on Mandeville Canyon in Brentwood. Once he was tucked in for the night, I went home to walk and talk with Winnie.

As I drove down Sunset to the freeway, I debated what to do about my follower if they were still following me: Ditch them? Confront them? Or let it be? They already had my address so by driving home I wasn't giving them any new information. If I confronted them, maybe Lucky would be there to back me up. That was one too many maybes for my liking.

I let it be and drove home to see what awaited me there.

CHAPTER SIXTY

Do Not Disturb

YOU KNOW THAT feeling when you know you've forgotten something and it's too late to do anything about it? I felt bad. I'd forgotten that Candy had explicitly told me she needed to speak to me when the expo closed for the night.

I've been accused of not thinking/caring enough about others and being wrapped up in myself. I want to think that's not entirely true, but it's not entirely untrue either.

Aw, shit is what I said to myself as I made the U-turn on Sunset and sped back to Pacific Coast Highway and Malibu. It gave me plenty of time to question my motives. Was I going to the swingers' party because I wanted to swing or because I wanted to check in with Candy? I'd detected a note of concern when she'd asked to speak to me, and she was a member of our disturbed-aura group. I wouldn't feel okay if I went home and something bad happened to her. Even if I'm not as concerned with others as I could be, I do have to answer to me.

The person collecting money at the door wasn't inclined to let me in to see Candy. They'd heard it all before. I asked the guy to notify Candy that David from Eve's Tantric Garden was here.

I waited, and watched who was coming to the party. As Rajiv

had said, it was predominately middle-aged couples sexily attired and soon to be sexily unattired. I was pleased that no one evoked any urgency on my part to follow them inside. A well-muscled guy whispered in the door guy's ear and he beckoned me over.

"Possibly she's in one of the bedrooms. He'll check again."

I tried not to horribilize. Rajiv had said she'd spent the previous night behind closed doors so I'd focus on her being alive doing whatever she was doing as opposed to what I feared.

Fifteen minutes later, the muscled guy returned.

"Door's still locked, which means Do Not Disturb. You can keep waiting or go home and try again next weekend."

My body was tired, my mind was racing, and Winnie was waiting.

I drove home. The black Camaro had come with me. It made me nervous and I hurried into the house.

Winnie hasn't got it within her to attack anyone, but she is large and might scare someone off. After a hearty greeting, we went outside for a walk and I was relieved to see that the Camaro had gone, but I was still uneasy.

CHAPTER SIXTY-ONE
Wake-up Call

Sunday, August 11, 1985

ONE OF THE things I like about Winnie is her height. She can rest her head on the side of the bed and stare eye to eye with me. Sometimes she jumps up and snuggles up next to me. She weighs in at one-twenty so her presence is useful training for when someone else might sleep there. I just hope they won't be as restless and that they wash more frequently, although that's on me.

This too-early-in-the-morning, she was eye to eye with me and barking. Had the possum come in the kitchen, or had a different intruder awoken Winnie?

Although I have my quotient of paranoid concerns, my home-invasion protection is a Louisville Slugger that used to get me some hits as a kid. My house is built over various levels to accommodate the hillside, and the bedroom is on the lowest. Winnie might be my best friend, but I had her go up the stairs first anyway.

She was no more eager than me. She kept turning her head and staring at me as if to reassure herself we were in this together. The house is small enough that as soon as I reached the top step, I could see the main area was clear. The only other room they would be in was the kitchen.

Winnie isn't much of a fetcher, but she will chase one of her toys a time or two if I throw it. I retrieved a ball from the bedroom and threw it toward the kitchen. Her scampering over there would either flush out the intruder or encourage them to leave. She brought it back, and I grabbed the Slugger and inched my way forward. I threw the ball around the kitchen corner and Winnie scurried after it. I came in behind her.

A possum was standing in the middle of the floor. If you've ever heard the phrase "playing possum" I can tell you what that means. Despite our presence in the room, the possum stood its ground. Winnie and I have experienced this before.

I grabbed the broom from the closet—my tool of choice in this situation—and swept the possum out the door. I was relieved, but being followed the previous evening had set my nerves on edge. Winnie's too, it seemed.

After that invigorating wake-up call, I settled down to oatmeal, blueberries, and a banana and tackled the Sunday edition of the *LA Times*. The Woo-Woo Death Expo had made the front page again. Vendors would be busy.

There were few details about Saffron's demise. As had been the case with the other victims, no cause of death was listed. There was also speculation about the UFO guys having contracted a fatal virus, or another poisonous element being in play.

I channeled Madame Vadama, laid my cards on the table, and read them. Today was the last day of the expo. I saw a reveal in my future. I didn't see what would get the truth out but the expo would close at four so that's when I'd do my thing.

I'd need to get our disturbed-aura group in the Love Doctor's booth—it had the most open space. I'd have to ask her, which would give me the opportunity to find out how she felt about being stood up. I wasn't looking forward to it. If I could pull off the reveal in her

"Hello again. I was hoping to see you before things picked up, but you're already getting an early start."

"Hello again. That was Alexandra from Mystic Jewelry. You ought to go check out her necklaces. Perhaps get one for the Love Doctor."

"Would it aid my cause? I'm kinda in the doghouse."

"It wouldn't hurt. I'm glad you're here. I have a question for you."

"Go for it. I only have a little time though, and I do want to run something by you as well."

"Then let's get to it. The person I've been talking with you about is coming soon and I was hoping for another suggestion. She tried the technique you suggested and he gave ground. She wants more. If you help me with that, I'd be happy to help you."

"I do have a suggestion," I said, nodding. "It's a bit risky, but she's on a roll and it's time for her to double down. She has more power than she realizes. Often people lord their power over others out of fear that the others are more powerful. I'm guessing he puts her down so she won't feel secure enough to leave him. He might even have her followed because he's afraid she's cheating… if she is, don't tell me. This is the time to get him to own up to how much he values her."

"Are you suggesting she threatens to leave?"

"No. I don't advise that kind of power play. I have a way that will increase her power, make them both happier, and enhance your credibility."

"You do?"

"I do. I'm willing to bet he thinks she doesn't have a head for business."

"To be truthful" —she lowered her voice— "she doesn't."

"That's fine. We can help with that."

"We can?"

"Here's what I suggest. You gaze into the future and see a movie… no wait, you see many movies."

"Did I tell you he was a producer?"

"No, you didn't, but I too have mystical powers. You explain to her that these movies are fuzzy because it looks like the golden goose might be about to have their wings clipped. His instincts for picking the best projects, along with the best woman to marry, are excellent. But if he doesn't trust and let go of some control he could lose everything."

"I'm not sold. Don't you have another technique you can give me?"

"I do but you're missing the point. I'm assuming he doesn't hold psychics in the highest esteem and undervalues you like he does his wife. If you get her to give him business advice, it will enhance her position and yours."

I could tell she liked that, but her forehead wrinkled.

"What makes you so sure he wants to subdue the golden goose?"

"Movie people are afraid to say yes. It's easier to say no to a project and not be associated with its failure than to risk putting it on the line. Chances are he has a project lined up. And if he fully supports it, the odds of it succeeding are improved. Just like if he fully supports her, the odds of their marriage succeeding will increase. You don't trim the feathers of the golden goose because that can kill it."

"I get it. He needs to believe in her and whatever project he has lined up and not cut them off at the feet."

"That's it. Now I have to go."

"What about that thing you wanted my help with?"

"I can handle it. If not, I'll swing by later."

CHAPTER SIXTY-THREE
The Meeting

"I HAVE IT together," said Bennett. "They'll cut scenes, add a character or two. Heck, I might have done that if I'd written one more draft."

"That's very balanced of you," I said. "You told me that when your editor takes out hunks of your waxing about this or that, you get cranky. You can see the value of the edits, but you liked those riffs. You just have to remember that if they're going to translate your book to a movie, they no doubt have experience with what makes for a successful movie."

"No, they don't. These guys are money guys. Not movie guys. They like to be the bosses. That's all. I get it—the fuckers have me by the balls. They can take a scene or two, but I want to finish the script, direct it, and have my cameo, like Alfred Hitchcock did. That's what I want and that's what we mostly agreed to."

"It's where the mostly is that'll be the problem," Lucky said.

Louise put her hand on Bennett's driving force. "Honey, they'll squeeze your balls, and not in an arousing way. I'll do that. Remember, we got the team here, so we got them outnumbered. And between us, we can out-maneuver them. Let's not blow it up when they squeeze."

"I agree," I said. "Try to just listen, note what's being said and how it's being said, and tell them you'll consider it and get back to them. Then, when we're alone, you can huff and puff and blow the house down. But first let's listen. Be mellow. Hear them out. Then we'll brainstorm what to do later. What do you think? Can you do that?"

"That sounds abundantly appropriate, and if I were an appropriate person I'd follow that advice. I've gotten where I've gotten by not being appropriate so I'm not inclined to be so now," he said, and took out a vial of coke. He snorted a generous amount and passed it to Louise, who was holding her own. She passed it to Lucky, who took a morning pick-me-up and passed it to me. I handed it back to Bennett.

I've basically elected to leave my coke years behind me before they leave me behind. I suppose under irresistible circumstances I'd fall off the wagon, but not this morning, not when I wanted to be on my A game.

"I do hear you," Bennett said. "I'm listening, and we'll see what happens. Now let's all go in there and beat the shit out of those fuckers."

Rip opened the door and welcomed us, which was comforting in a weird way, even though it evened up the numbers a little. Yes, he worked for them, but he liked and trusted me. Yet I'd also seen him shoot someone and he'd make mincemeat of me if it ever came to that.

He escorted us into the producer's study. High ceiling, big fireplace, movie posters on the wall, a large desk with Mr. Russo behind it. Caddy stood beside him. There were two empty chairs in front. Behind Mr. Russo, a glass wall looked out onto the golf course and the mountains beyond.

"Good morning, gentlemen," Bennett said. He strode up and shook their hands, nice and friendly. They were in the movie business together—why not try to be collaborative rather than combative?

Bennett and Louise took the two chairs. Lucky stood next to

Louise and I parked myself by Bennett. Rip stood behind us. We said our hellos but that was it for the foreplay. No small talk about the Dodgers or the weather.

"We have an update," Caddy said. "We're having someone else finish the script and direct the movie."

"What the fuck are you saying?" Bennett said. "We already agreed to all this. You can't do that. We have a contract."

"Yes, we do have a contract. Read it sometime. You've broken the terms so you've forfeited your rights."

"What the fuck? We already dealt with this in Palm Springs. I haven't broken the terms of the contract since then."

"That we don't know. We do know you forfeited your right to write the script and direct when you fucked up before."

"We've already been over this. You guys are trying to stab me in the fucking back. What the fuck is going on here?"

"We agreed you'd retain your share of the profits. We didn't agree you'd write the script and direct."

"When we agreed before it was about everything. Not just the money."

"You're no longer writing the script or directing the movie or doing the cameo. Go home, wait for your check, and don't get caught doing coke."

Bennett went quiet, which was odd. It wasn't like him to sit in a chair and act appropriately. Yet neither had he said anything about how he'd heard them and would consider it and get back to them.

In *A Lesson in Cowboys and Murder*, I used a therapeutic technique called doubling, where I stood behind the suspects and said out loud what I thought they would be saying if they weren't holding it in. It can move things along.

"I don't want to speak for Bennett, but what I think he wants to say is that he hears what you're saying, is nonplussed by it, and will be leaving soon. He'll get back to you shortly with his response."

"That what you think, Bennett?" asked Caddy.

"It is, you fucking assholes. You guys really piss me off. Why the fuck are you fucking with me? You bought my book because you knew it would be a blockbuster, yet you don't trust me to take it to the bank. What the fuck? I'm a successful writer. A very fucking successful writer. Just because I've never written a fucking movie doesn't mean I can't. Everyone arrives a virgin. I've got more talent in my asshole then you guys have in your fucking heads. So, yeah, I hear your fucking tight-assed stupid request and I'll talk to my fucking people and we'll get back to you."

With that, he got up to leave.

Mr. Russo finally spoke. I wished he hadn't.

"Dr. Unger needs to stay."

CHAPTER SIXTY-FOUR
Some Words

SINCE I WAS a kid I've had fantasies about being singled out. Being the recipient of an award. Giving a speech. Being asked to stay behind with Mr. Russo, Caddy, and Rip while the rest of my posse rode off was not the stuff of my fantasy life. I watched them leave and braced myself.

"Dr. Unger, we need to have words with you," Caddy said.

"Why don't I sit down so we can discuss what's on your minds?"

"Do you have anything you want to tell us? It'll be easier for you if you tell us."

"I'm all about talking. What exactly are we talking about?"

"We're talking about Mrs. Russo."

"I haven't met Mrs. Russo. If I did, I'm sure I'd find her delightful."

"What do you know?"

"Do you have a picture of her? Maybe I'd recognize her. Names are not my strong suit."

The producer turned a silver-framed picture on the desk toward me. It was the woman who'd been seeing Madame Vadama and whose picture I'd seen at his place in Palm Springs.

"I've seen her at the Whole Life Expo. I've been spending time there the past few days."

"What does she do there?"

"Rip, no doubt, has a better idea than me. I tend to stay in the same area all day but I've seen her strolling around a couple of times."

"Strolling around alone or with someone?"

"Alone. She spoke to a woman a time or two. That's all I can recall. Anything else before I go?"

"We're not done. What woman?"

"Rip, can you help me out here? She might have spoken with the fortune teller, Madame Vadama."

"Tell us the rest."

"The rest? That's all I know."

"Tell us why you followed Madame Vadama here."

"Oh, that. That's another story."

"Let's hear it."

"You might have read about it in the paper. The woo-woo deaths. This will sound odd, but it's a woo-woo thing. There's a group of booths next to each other at the expo that have disturbed auras, which portends bad things. Yeah, it's weird, but that's what they believe. Get this—in our group, there have been three deaths under mysterious circumstances. And I'm in that group, so I've been trying to keep tabs on everyone."

"So what?"

"So Madame Vadama is in our disturbed-aura group. I followed her to see what she was up to and she came here, stayed a bit, and returned to the Civic. That's it."

"She the killer?"

"I'd be surprised, but it's possible. I can't discern any overlap between group members aside from the clustering of our booth locations. I have no clue regarding motive, means, or much of anything. That's why I followed her; I was hoping it would lead to something."

"What did it lead to?"

"It led to your wanting to talk to me."

"We're done now."

"Before I go, there's something I want to say. You're making a mistake with Bennett. Heck, we all make them. Bennett surely does. But look at him. You can't not look at him when he's in the room. He commands attention whether you want to give it to him or not. That's what he'll do with your movie. I told you this before—he's number one on the *New York Times* Bestseller before the books even come out, because he writes compelling stories, and, like him or not, you can't ignore him. He's a sure thing. The golden goose. Why not ride it?"

CHAPTER SIXTY-FIVE

Sunshine in Siberia

WE'VE ALL TRIED to plant a seed in someone's mind at one time or another. You want them to think you're all that or buy your product or follow your political beliefs. There are numerous ways to influence. I do it overtly and covertly as there's a time and a place for each. If I laid the ground for Bennett being the golden goose, and Mrs. Russo then came home and said the same thing, well, maybe he'd think it was a woo-woo message he couldn't ignore.

The posse was waiting in Bennett's black Mercedes 380 SL convertible. It was a snazzy car. Unfortunately, Lucky had to snuggle in the back, a space not really intended for anyone older than ten.

"Doc, everything like sunshine in Siberia?" he said.

"You tell me. For us to see the sun, we're going to need a bit of cooperation. Can we do that?"

"Certainly," Louise said. "You can do that, Bennie, can't you?"

"Yes, my dear. If that makes you happy. But I'm pissed at those dickheads. I had my lawyer cousin double-check the contract. They're full of shit."

"Their lawyers might have outmaneuvered yours. Or maybe they'll work it out on the back end. Yes, rant and rave and then we'll figure out how to respond. But first I need your help."

"What are you talking about?"

"The reveal. It's today at four at the Love Doctor's booth. I don't want you directly involved, not at first. I'd rather you casually make your way to standing at the edge. There'll be a moment when I need to involve you in a big way, but I'm unclear when to spring that at the moment."

"Like at my cousin Geto's wedding when the cows came home from the field."

"Yeah, like that."

"What are you planning to do, Doc?" Louise asked.

"I'll get the group together and see if I can mix things up so that the woo-woo gets flowing and something pops up."

"That would never happen in one of my books," Bennett said.

"That's why yours are bestsellers."

"Anything else you need from us?" Louise said.

"I might need Lucky's time midday if that works for you."

"We'll be fine, Doc," she said. "Bennett will be a good naughty boy, and when he snorts up, he needs to go into a stall and stay low. Isn't that right, Bennie?"

"Yes, my love. But soon I gotta let off some steam."

CHAPTER SIXTY-SIX

Where's the Profit?

ON THE DRIVE to the Civic, I wondered if the *LA Times* article had bumped up attendance. It wouldn't surprise me if the expo was busier and Dennis happier.

Hmm. One of the threads you search for when there's a murder is who profits. Clearly he did. But, then, so did everybody else. There had to be less lethal ways to make money, though plenty have been killed in pursuit of it.

To choose murder as a means to earn money indicates a high degree of desperation and pathology. In our case, it was desperation and pathology that someone was managing to hide but that had to be boiling just below the surface.

I don't doubt that the vast majority of us when threatened would kill to defend ourselves. Desperate times bring desperate measures. We might well be haunted for the rest of our lives even if we felt we'd had no real choice, but it's do or be done in. The killer/s at the expo had found a way of justifying their actions in their mind.

If money was the motive, there'd be a trail the police could follow. I'd need a path that would encourage the killer to reveal their concerns. Next to sharing the truth about our sex lives, most of us opt for privacy when it comes to the specifics of how we deal with money. Sharing the existence of money woes is one thing; the details and the depth of the worry, well, that's harder.

If following the money trail was too challenging, what else could go on the list of motivations? Rage? Jealousy? Envy? Attention? The thrill of it? Could be any one of those or something else. But whatever it was, it was deeply personal, locked in at the core of that person's being.

And I needed a way to set it free.

CHAPTER SIXTY-SEVEN
Stealing from Us

I WAS ANXIOUS to get to the expo and check out whether Candy was there along with the rest of the crew. She was. The attendance was already greater than it had been the day before and the tantric-sex booth was surrounded by people clamoring to see where the woo-woo deaths had gone down. I wanted to ask Phillippe about Connected Pictures but he was chatting with a group of women and didn't look like he'd be available any time soon. Candy also had a small audience but I waved and got her attention, and she excused herself and came over.

"Where have you been?" she asked. "I'm glad to see you. I was worried about you."

"I was worried about you too. I'm sorry we haven't had time to talk about Saffron. You holding up all right?"

"I'm managing. If we didn't have so much invested I'd have packed up and gone home."

"I hear you. I wanted to make it last night but I got tied up. I drove out to Malibu and asked after you, but they said you were in one of the bedrooms and couldn't disturb you."

She glared at me.

"Oh, Rajiv told me where the house is."

Okay, I lied. I don't like lying, but in this case it was smarter than admitting that I'd followed her there. Of course, if she checked with Rajiv, I'd lose whatever credibility I had with both of them.

"Too bad you couldn't get in. Another time. I only have a minute. As you can see, we're swamped, but I do want to run something by you."

"Go for it."

"This may or may not be relevant, but since you're trying to find out whodunit it might help to know this: I suspect Dennis is stealing from us."

"Really? That's distressing. How do you think he's doing it?"

"Merchants are supposed to be getting ten percent of the gate. I think he's underreporting the numbers. Everyone is paying cash, so either he's skimming off the top or the box office staff are stuffing their pockets."

I preferred to think Dennis was lining his own pockets; it gave me one more reason not to like him. And I'd already been considering how he'd profit from the publicity the deaths had generated. Maybe snagging the admission fees indicated he really did have money problems and was working more than one angle.

As pleased as I was, I was struck by Candy's reaction to the whole situation. Two of her business partners had been killed yet she was still staffing the booth and disappearing off to Malibu to do whatever she was doing behind closed doors.

I've never had that kind dedication to my work, which might explain why Dennis had the radio show and Candy could rent the fancy house.

CHAPTER SIXTY-EIGHT

Is It Worth It?

BUSINESS WAS BOOMING. I couldn't see Dennis, but given the high attendance levels and the possible skimming he ought to have been feeling pretty chipper. Later I'd check in with Eve and see how our auras were coming along. Hopefully, they'd lightened up. I hadn't yet touched base with Nova since standing her up, and while I wasn't looking forward to hearing my fate, I'd practiced enough speeches to have talked myself into believing I'd be granted a second chance. First on my list, though, was Herb's Herbology, and a consultation with the man himself.

Herb had the appearance of someone you might expect to be well acquainted with the kind of herbs you smoke—dreadlocks, scraggy beard, Grateful Dead T-shirt. I wasn't convinced he had what I needed but it wouldn't hurt to ask. He had jars of proper herbs and a selection of stone pipes one could use to smoke the other type. Two Birkenstock-wearing, hashish-smelling guys were already with him but they soon drifted off and I greeted him with a smile.

"Hi there. I hope you can help me."

"That's my purpose."

"If I needed to conjure up a concoction that would instantly kill a person, what would you recommend?"

"Dude," he said, stepping back. "Chill out. Whoever's bugging you has their own devils."

"Don't we all. But let me assure you, I'm not a killer. I'm trying to find out what killed the people in the other aisle. Any idea?"

"That's a relief, man, but—and I don't mean any offense—you shouldn't have that information. If you're that mad, you should go see the Love Doctor."

"I'm sorry you don't trust me. Everyone's a bit on edge. And here I am, asking how to kill someone. I'm not good at foreplay."

"What?"

"Nothing. Just tell me. Are there any plants that if ingested would kill a person on the spot?"

"As I said, knowing which roots and flowers could accomplish that is not information you ought to have. Now, excuse me, I need to talk to this other person."

I'm not usually suspected of murder right away. I needed to keep working on the foreplay.

I returned to our disturbed aisle and was drifting down it with a headful of excuses for Nova when One called out to me from the UFO booth.

"Dr. Unger, could you come over here for a minute? This couple has been asking about the secret of extraterrestrial sex and we think they'd be encouraged if they heard from you." He turned to his customers-to-be. "Dr. Unger has awareness of the secret."

"Happy to provide a testimonial as to its potency. These two brave souls have traveled to far-away places and come across things we can't even imagine. They will disclose the secret for a price because they're using the money to further the cause of relationships with a universe we can barely comprehend."

"That's a noble cause," said a rather frail man. "But did it work? Have you tried it out and is it worth it?"

"Did it work? I can only partially answer that because I have yet to be with a person in such a way that I could verify the impact of the secret in a fully meaningful way. That said, I have verified the essence of the secret with a person I wish to engage more meaningfully with, and I can bear witness that, so far, things are as proceeding quite well."

"So you haven't actually had sex with anyone?"

"Well, not since I learned the secret. However, the foreplay has been extraterrestrially based and well received."

"So was it worth twenty dollars?"

"To me? Yes. To you, I can't answer that. We all value things differently. If you learn the secret and apply it, you'll learn your lesson."

A big problem with lying is that one bad thing can lead to another bad thing. I'd lied to Candy about Rajiv disclosing the address, and now I'd stretched the truth regarding extraterrestrial sex. Then again, I hadn't touched Nova, so technically I was employing the technique. Was I experiencing a heightened level of pleasure because of it? Well, I was very excited. But, honestly, when I was with her, I hoped we'd move on and have some old-fashioned down-to-earth sex.

CHAPTER SIXTY-NINE

Past Lives

SHERIDAN CAME OUT into the aisle and pointed toward the entrance. "Dave, can you come with me? Got a couple of boxes of stuff in the car and would welcome your lending a hand."

We left the building and walked to the parking lot.

"We spent all night making stuff to sell," he said. "Everything's flying off the shelves."

"You've hit the mother lode, that's great. But has Eve seen any shifts in our auras? Are things picking up for us?"

"Money-wise, yes. Life-wise, no. She's been worrying that anger from a previous life is manifesting itself."

"Hold on. In regard to whose previous life?"

"Well, according to Eve, everyone's. If you believe in past lives, we've all got leftover stuff that we carry. You can try to balance it out in the next life, but then something else pops up."

"You believe that?"

We arrived at a late-sixties baby-blue and white VW bus.

"Cool wheels. Yours or hers?"

"Eve's. She's a hippie."

"Yeah. She's value-driven, although her capitalist roots are showing. But come on, do you believe in past lives? The closest I've come is experiencing that sense of having been someplace before even if it's my first time."

"Yeah, I get those déjà vu moments, but I file those in the Let's Not Think About It department."

"I've got things piled up in that department as well. Overthinking them could cause a significant disruption to my tenuous relationship with what I hold as reality."

"Big time. I avoid dwelling on the woo-woo as well. But Eve, she's not afraid of it. She embraces it. And she feels more leftover anger coming forth."

"That's troubling, but it reminds me… I'm planning on asking all of our disturbed-aura group to meet in the Love Doctor's booth after the expo closes at four. Any help you can provide would be appreciated. It's not an optimal time; everybody will be focused on tearing down their booth, grabbing a drink, or just going home. But we need to meet quickly so I can impart lifesaving news that'll make most everyone happier."

"You know who's behind the deaths?"

"In a different life. In the here and now, I'm not yet clear. But an idea's forming about how we can change that."

CHAPTER SEVENTY

Embracing Life

THERE WAS THAT lying thing again. Technically, it was true—I'd started to consider how we might reveal whodunit. Truthfully though, I was counting on unforeseen woo-woo to pull me through.

We arrived back at the booth and Sheridan unpacked the boxes. Prior to the publicity surrounding the deaths, attendees had window-shopped more and bought less. Now, it was the other way around, as if they wanted a souvenir from the Woo-Woo Death Expo.

I glanced over at the Love Doctor's booth. Nova wasn't there. I didn't panic, but the urge to horribilize was coming on. I badly wanted to ask Eve if she knew where Nova was, but she was busy and Sheridan had slipped off.

Madame Vadama's booth was bustling too, though she managed to give me a knowing look that I'd need to follow up on later. The one person who wasn't cashing in was Rajiv. The parade kept passing by his booth. I'm no expert, but the way I saw it his chakra needed tuning again. I headed his way and bade him good morning.

"It is for many. As you can see, it's not for me."

"Same problem? You don't feel deserving of pleasure?"

"I feel nothing. I have no creative energy. All are wise to stay away."

"No one's ever accused me of being wise. A wise-ass, yes. Wise? No. So what's going on?"

"I went to Malibu last night."

"I went too. I was looking for Candy but didn't go in."

"She was behind the closed door again. It was very disappointing."

"I'm sure. Plus, the second time often isn't quite so exciting."

"That's true, but I had plenty of excitement. Possibly too much."

"You mean like the kind where you wet your pants or where you ejaculate too soon?"

"No no. My performance was an improvement on the previous night. I was too excited in a different way."

"Care to tell me?"

"I am ashamed. I understand why Candy and Phillippe needed to go to the house. It's their business. But I didn't have to go. I could have found a more respectful way to mourn Saffron's loss, but—and I shouldn't admit this—it aroused me. Please don't misunderstand, I don't mean her death. I mean that the life force within me said to live my life while I still have it."

"Yeah, I can understand that. One approach to mourning her life—a nice, proper way—might have been somber and subdued. But you chose another. And perhaps Saffron's spirit was in the house and you honored her in a way she might have connected with."

Before I asked if he'd seen Nova, we were interrupted by a customer. I'd like to believe our conversation helped tune up his chakra but I left the booth unbalanced. While embracing life in the face of death made sense, I couldn't shake the knowledge that killers can be aroused by their actions. I parked that thought and left Rajiv to his fate.

CHAPTER SEVENTY-ONE
To Go

NOVA WASN'T AT her booth, which bothered me. She'd come to the expo to work it, and she wasn't. Or at least not in any way I could see. I reminded myself that the other deaths had taken place in our disturbed neighborhood; the fact that she wasn't here meant she'd be okay, didn't it?

Or had my standing her up meant she couldn't face being here? She told me she'd already been dumped once yesterday. Maybe being so beautiful and desired had given her a glass jaw. No, that was absurd. Even I wasn't so swept up in me to believe that was feasible.

Eve waved me over. "Your aura is still dark, but you're not alone. Sheridan told me you'd been asking whether things have changed. Unfortunately we're all sucking energy. I've tried to cleanse our auras but it's like we're all stuck. I'd focus harder on it but we're so busy at the moment that I don't even have time to talk. Could you get us a sandwich?"

"Write down what you want and I'll get it. Before I go, have you seen Nova?"

"Yes, she was here earlier. She's miffed at you. I only spoke with her briefly. She asked me what was up with you."

"I hope you spoke to the brighter side of my auras."

"I told her the truth. Just get the same as yesterday, but have them put the coleslaw on the side. And bring pickles."

I wanted her to share what she'd said to Nova, but she returned to her customers and I was left hanging. Sheridan had said she was displeased with me because of how I portrayed her in my music book. I didn't want that displeasure to shape the current narrative, but was worried that it had. I'd find out soon enough from Nova... if she'd even talk with me.

The good news was, she was alive. The bad news was, she was miffed and probably not that eager to become unmiffed.

I was grinding on that when Dennis strode toward the end of the aisle and past the tantric-sex booth. Not even a twitch of faux concern appeared on his face, he had a little skip in his step. The killings were big business.

I made a note to ask Eve if she'd gotten a look at his aura.

I took up one of my favorite expo exploits: I followed him. I'd followed others in our disturbed-aura group; I might as well see what he was up to... just as long as it didn't delay my food run.

During my time in the Navy when we were in port, food trucks would drive out to the pier. We called them roach coaches, which might be an indicator of the quality therein. If you wanted someone to get you something you'd say, "I'll buy, you fly." I'd flown and bought for Eve and Sheridan and was about to do it again. They'd told me they'd pay me for my time at the expo, but if lunch was anything to go by, it wouldn't be in any way that I could buy a sandwich with.

Dennis knocked on a door marked *Box Office*, the door opened, and he entered. I scurried over and peeked through the glass. He was handed what appeared to be a bag of money. Then he got into a big argument with the man who was supervising those collecting the admission fee. If money-skimming was in play, was there an accomplice?

CHAPTER SEVENTY-TWO
Use the Booth

THEY SAY IT takes money to make money. Whether I'd make anything from buying sandwiches for everyone in our group sans Dennis remained to be seen. However, I'd figured they all were busy, would appreciate the gesture, and it might make them more inclined to attend the four o'clock meetup. And hopefully Nova would forgive me and agree to hang out with me after the meeting.

I got everyone the same sandwich: turkey with lettuce, tomato, Dijon, and no mayo. Coleslaw and pickles on the side. I have a tendency to overcomplicate things so I was endeavoring to keep lunch simple. Unfortunately, Phillippe was a vegetarian, Candy didn't like turkey, Rajiv was a vegan, and the UFOs were on a plant-based diet. So far so bad. Madame Vadama was grateful and told me to come back when I'd finished my deliveries. Eve and Sheridan were thankful for the fare, though not enough to pay for it.

That left me with five extra sandwiches, plus mine and Nova's. At least she was in her booth. I caught her eye but received no indication of how she was feeling vis-à-vis me. I got in line behind two college-aged boys.

"Guys, can you help me with something?"

"What's that?"

"I've got extra turkey sandwiches if you're interested, but you can't eat them here. I'll give them to you if you go eat them someplace else and then come back and see the Love Doctor later."

"You trying to bribe us so you can see her first?"

"I'm hoping. Interested?"

"Hand 'em over."

The college kids left and I gave Nova my best forgive-me smile.

"I come bearing gifts," I said.

"It's a start."

"You like turkey on rye with Dijon?"

"It'll do. What happened to you? I don't take kindly to being stood up."

"All I can say, although I will say more, is I was trying to protect you."

"From you? Do I need to know anything before I eat this?"

"I trust the sandwich is okay, and possibly Eve vouched for me. I was sleuthing—trying to discover what happened to our neighbors. I wanted to tell you I'd be late but—"

"That sounds reasonable. And yet Rajiv told me that last night you were at a swinger's party in Malibu."

"I hope he told you I was outside the party, not inside it. I was trying to touch base with Candy from the tantric-sex booth because she'd been quite agitated and had asked to speak with me before I left the expo. I clean forgot."

"Let me get this straight. Last night, you were sleuthing and went to a party looking for Candy but didn't go in."

"It's complicated. I could have gone in. And while it might have been erotic to be there, at the moment I'm practicing an extraterrestrial sex secret."

"What are you talking about?"

"That was kind of a joke. The UFO guys are peddling a sex secret they encountered on their space travels and the technique seems to come naturally to me."

"Should I be happy for you?"

"I don't think so. Please accept my apology. Come on, it's not a secret that I'm smitten with you. I wouldn't have stood you up unless it really was a critical situation."

"I'll consider letting you off the hook, especially since you skipped the mayo, but I'm not as interested as I was before."

"But you haven't lost all interest."

"Some, yes. Not all."

"So is there a chance for redemption tonight?"

"Let's see how things turn out. Eve told me you intend to use my booth later. Want to discuss that?"

"I hope I didn't overstep the mark. There's a small group of us with disturbed auras and I want the group to meet at four. Your booth has the least furniture, so it would be the easiest to use. I intended to run it by you first but I bumped into Sheridan before I got to you, who told Eve, who told you. Did she tell you I planned to run it by you first?"

"She told me a few things about you—some of which I'd already inferred—but, no, she didn't tell me you were going to ask permission before you went ahead."

"I don't usually have to resort to this, but I'm trying to court you and not getting very far, so you need to know that I'm a big proponent of asking permission. It's in my first book."

"I've read a couple of your books. I don't remember that."

"You have? You didn't tell me. Did you like them? Well, more importantly, do you like me? Do I still have a chance?"

"Let's wait and see on that. And, yes, it's fine to use the booth."

CHAPTER SEVENTY-THREE
Freedom or Death

"YOU MAKING ANY progress with Nova?" Madame Vadama asked.

"I want to think so, but I'm not sure. You see anything in our future?"

"The picture is hazy."

"Have you been consulting with a Magic 8-Ball?"

"One does not need a toy to see that your future with her is murky. You should follow the advice you give."

"I talk it better than I walk it. How did things go this morning?"

"Like you, I don't necessarily follow advice. I've planted a seed with her. We shall see how soon it breaks ground."

"I don't mean to pry—well, I do mean to pry— but can you tell me if you used the term golden goose and if you think she'll repeat it?"

"And why is this of interest to you? I thought you were sharing out of the goodness of your heart. Like with the sandwich. But is there duplicity in your heart?"

"Yes and no. My heart wants a happy ending. Stop the killing, solve the whodunit, and get the girl. That's it. But how I get there? Well, it's a winding road with bad turns, side roads taken, and no clear end in sight."

"And the golden goose plays a part in this?"

"Yes and no. I hoped to plant an idea in someone's head and if it comes from multiple sources it might sink in. Ideally, they'll have an ah-ha moment and realize they're being penny wise and pound foolish. They need to free the golden goose, not kill it. That's what I'm hoping for."

"Freedom or death, that is the basis of life."

"Yeah, that plays out in a multitude of ways throughout our lives. It's a powerful dynamic. In the interests of keeping our freedom, I have a favor to ask."

"Another?"

"That's what relationships are about. You do this, I do that."

"What do you want?"

"I want you to get your client and her husband here before four. I'm asking you, Rajiv, Candy, Phillippe, the UFO guys, Dennis, Eve, Sheridan, and Nova to meet with me for a few minutes at four."

She raised her eyebrows. "For what purpose?"

"I've gazed into my crystal ball. That's when whodunit will be revealed."

CHAPTER SEVENTY-FOUR

The Golden Goose

MADAME VADAMA WASN'T convinced she could get Mr. and Mrs. Russo to come to the expo but said she'd give it a try. She didn't have time to consult her cards regarding how that would turn out. And since I didn't have a Magic 8-Ball, I'd have to go with the flow.

I'd told her I wanted Mr. Russo to hear "golden goose" from multiple sources because you hear something once, you ignore it; twice, you note it; three times, you're curious.

There are moments in life when we have to stand up in front of others and define ourselves—show what we're made of and why we deserve our due. There are also times when we have to take a back seat.

If Mr. Russo and his wife showed up, and the big reveal came out the way I hoped, I'd manufacture a way to highlight Bennett. I wanted the producer to witness the value of Bennett's being alive and free to live his life his own way and get headlines. I wanted tomorrow's *LA Times* to read "Woo-woo expo murderer exposed by famous mystery writer Bennett Price." With that headline, the producer might back off from trying to clip Bennett's wings.

The posse showed up. Bennett in a pink polo shirt, khaki pants, and Top-Siders; Lucky in a Hawaiian shirt, shorts, and sandals;

Louise in black cowboy boots, a tight purple T-shirt that showed off her curves, and a short denim skirt that showed off the rest.

They'd been up all weekend and were wired, twitchy, and off-kilter. I could work with that. You have to take what you get.

We went outside and stood under a palm tree.

"I need your help. Hopefully by helping me you'll be helping you. And when I say you, I mean Bennett. If you do well, we'll all do well."

"Louise said to listen to you. I can't always be a good boy and Louise needs to punish me when I'm not. If we can help you and it helps me, I'm all in. But I'm ready to explode on those fuckers. They've got a fucking lot of nerve trying to push me out. Jesus fucking Christ."

"You have every reason to be furious. They're definitely fucking with you, but I think I have a way to get them off your back."

"Swell. But, first, I have a question."

"Yes?"

"How long have you known about the swinger parties and why didn't you tell me? Jeez, that could have solved a lot of problems right there."

"We can go over that later, although I'll tell you now that no drugs are allowed. You'd have to hide it, and being with strangers wouldn't be safe. They could take pictures. You're better off fantasizing about that like the rest of us. Except Rajiv. He's one of the group I need your help with."

"So come on, Doc," Louise said. "Let's hear what you have up your sleeve."

"Yeah, we'll help you like Cousin Dancho helped get that mule out of the well."

"That's kind of you and him. I want to play two different tunes at the same time and harmonize them."

"Like a duet," Lucky said. "We can sing for you. How about *Up on the Roof?*"

"Maybe that wasn't an applicable metaphor. When we're done here, I want Lucky to go over to Mr. Russo's house and tell him that something heavy's going down at four and he needs to be here. Tell him it involves Bennett, the golden goose. Oh, yeah, and tell him to bring his wife."

"Bennett's the golden goose? Dancho once had a goose that chased him all the time."

"That's too bad. Don't mention Dancho. When you talk, casually mention that Bennett's a golden goose. I can explain later."

"That's the favor?" Bennett asked.

"That's part one of the favor. All three of you need to show up before four. Come and hang out at the edge of the Love Doctor's booth. I'll be in there with seven others. I want them focused on the group so don't draw attention to yourselves. I repeat: silent witnesses. I'm hoping Mr. Russo and his wife will be at the booth across from us. They'll see you. You wave hello, point to the Love Doctor's booth, and whisper to them that serious woo-woo's about to happen."

"Serious woo-woo?" Louise said. "What do you have in mind?"

"Not much. I'm hoping it will come to me. Here's the thing— there will be a moment when I point at you, Bennett, and that will be your cue to point at the killer. If we nail it, you'll be on the front page of the *LA Times*."

"I point at the killer?"

"I'll point at you and you'll point at them."

"Got it. Who am I pointing at?"

"I don't know yet. But you'll know."

"I'll know?"

"That's the woo-woo. I'll get the woo-woo going. I'll do whatever it is I do and at some point it'll be obvious who the killer is. I hope. And then you'll point at them."

"Dave," Bennett said, resting his hand on my shoulder, "you're aiming higher with this ending. You certain you can pull it off?

And, more importantly, make sure I'm able to point out the killer? Otherwise what they write about me in the paper won't endear you to me."

"Yeah, but, you know, all publicity is good publicity. I'm sure you'll nail it, but if you have any hesitancy and don't feel the full conviction, point back at me and I'll take it from there. In fact, just point at me anyway. Then I can point at Louise and you can point at Lucky and hopefully one of us will get it."

"Dave, you had it there for a bit, but you wussed out. You just point to me and make sure I know who to point at."

"Here's what we'll do. When I touch my chin, that's a sign that you need to count clockwise from my perspective. So if the third person on my left is the killer. I'll touch my chin, then my right ear lobe, my left, my right, and then stop. One, two, three. Get it?"

"Got it."

"Good."

CHAPTER SEVENTY-FIVE

Where's My Woo-Woo?

I'D GOTTEN CARRIED away. It's hard enough solving these mysteries without having to loop in Bennett. If he remembered the signals, he'd be on a possible path to the front page. He'd have a fun time there too, and Mr. Russo would see his value. Just as long as his pent-up rage and the cocaine didn't tilt the scales.

I was overly aware of everything I didn't know, but reliant on what I did. Two people in the tantric-sex booth and Dr. Ketchall had been poisoned. Their booths were in direct sight of each other. Perhaps Dr. Ketchall had witnessed something connected with Gordon's murder that demanded he be eliminated. And what about Saffron? Had she posed another threat? The UFOs had heard a noise before the expo opened; that could indicate that things weren't copacetic between the tantric practitioners. Had Phillippe or Candy killed their partners, and Dr. Ketchall been an unfortunate business expense?

Or someone might have had ill will toward Gordon, and the rest of the killings were loose ends.

Or Dr. Ketchall had been the initial target and the tantric-sex victims were the loose ends.

Or someone still had work to do, because we'd all done something to piss them off.

More ors than auras. And while the police might take a courtesy minute to listen to Eve, they wouldn't buy the disturbed-aura angle. They'd be investigating this step by step, killing by killing, and trying to find a trail.

That would be the sensible thing to do. Thorough and thoughtful approaches tend to yield viable results. The police have their skill set and I have mine. Madame Vadama uses her intuition and reads the cards. I rely on intuition and read the people.

All of which was fine. But what would I actually do? Once everyone had assembled, I'd need to create something we could do collectively to reveal the killer.

I needed to have a gimmick, a prop, an idea, something I could work with. Calling forth our various higher powers, extraterrestrial knowledge, and spirits to offer themselves was one thing, but then what?

Dave, walk the walk. Get in touch with your inner and outer woo-woo and be the light. Be the one. Be the many. Let the wisdom of the universe come to you.

I was talking it, but I wasn't walking it.

I do believe there's a part of every killer that wants to speak the truth about what they did and why. They want to reveal. They don't want the consequences, yet the weight they carry is its own burden. It's a burden they can usually carry, but put them in a group and the pressure builds. One person opens up and it isn't long before others do. I was counting on nudging the killer toward revealing themselves, either consciously or unconsciously, so that Bennett could point them out.

I'd have to go back to basics.

CHAPTER SEVENTY-SIX
Thanks for the Sandwich

I HUNG OUT in the aisle outside the tantric-sex booth, waiting to catch Candy's eye. Instead I caught Phillippe's.

"Didn't get to thank you for lunch. That was kind of you."

"You all were busy. I wanted to make things easier. Sorry I didn't ask first. There's a favor I want to ask of you and Candy. This has been a surreal event and I'm truly sorry for your losses but can the two of you join the rest of us for a brief meeting in the Love Doctor's booth at four?"

"Unfortunately, I have to take off as soon as we're done here."

"I know. We all do. However, before we go we need to confront the killer."

"You know who the killer is?"

"We've got it mostly figured out. We need to share information. That's why we need you and Candy there."

"I may not be able to make it. I'll tell Candy. Thanks again for the sandwich."

"You're welcome. By the way, the police have already said they'll be speaking with those who don't come to the meeting."

Okay, I lied again. While I dream of having sufficient draw for my invitations to be accepted, in reality I know better. Extra pressure had been required. Otherwise, I'd only have myself to reveal.

CHAPTER SEVENTY-SEVEN

All About Me

IT'S WEIRD HOW life works. Earlier, I'd focused and asked the woo-woo forces to light the way. And they had. Not a bright light, but a flicker. The only problem was, it was all about me.

No one had yet been able to ascertain the cause of death. I was confident the police would determine it but in the meantime I'd been considering it. From what I'd heard, the deaths had been sudden, which meant the victims had likely drunk or been injected with something that had knocked them out instantly. Herb hadn't wanted to pass along what might do that, but he'd implied that there were plants that could do the trick.

In the movies, the villain sneaks up behind their victim with a cloth full of chloroform. That could have happened, but I'm not convinced what they do in the movies transfers to real life.

My knowledge about the chemistry of knock-'em-out substances is zero, but I have some experience. This is the all-about-me part. I've written about it before because Hunter Thompson has written about it before.

Ibogaine.

It's a psychoactive substance whose use had been reported by African hunters. I'd come across it during my reading of *Fear and*

Loathing on the Campaign Trail '72 but assumed that Edmund Muskie's supposed use of the drug had been a joke.

But then it had been used to paralyze then kill musicians at a music festival, which I'd written about in *A Lesson in Music and Murder.*

I was struck by the woo-woo synchronicity of that. Could someone have read the music book and been inspired to get a hold of ibogaine, mix the drug in a New Age shake, and share a toast with their victims? Or did they simply shoot them up? Whatever the delivery mechanism, if ibogaine was in play, there was more afoot than I'd previously imagined.

I could imagine why the drug might hold appeal. It might well be the new drug of choice for those who choose to lie around all day. Taken in small doses it was akin to opium but in larger doses it paralyzed you or took you to a deeper resting place. A fatal dose could have been administered accidently if someone wasn't careful about what they were doing. That could occur once, but not three times. Plus, ibogaine isn't in everyone's medicine cabinet. Which means the murders had been planned. But by whom and why?

Eve wasn't happy with what I'd written about her in the music book. And it was her who'd invited me here. She'd been the one to declare that a group of us had disturbed auras, but it wasn't like I could see it to believe it. She could have set up the whole thing to show me up and shut me down. The ultimate bad review.

Candy had pointed out that I ought to know a thing or two about time. Had she read one of my books and known that my dissertation was about time? My name tag had told Madame Vadama who I was but how had she known I was a doctor of psychology? And then there was Nova, who'd read some of my books. I was wondering which ones. Only the music and mystery books had death by poison.

If someone had schemed to use ibogaine because they'd read it in the music book, they probably wouldn't tell me. Or would they?

"My student years in general and my quasi-fraternity Dreamer beer mug in particular."

"Dave is certainly a dreamer. Beware if you're so bold as to date this fanciful man."

"Thanks for the heads-up," Nova said. "I knew something was up when he got all those sandwiches. That's dreamer territory."

"He rescued us," Eve said, giving me a hug. "Although your work is not finished."

"You don't seem to have much to pack up," Nova said. "You've been very busy."

"Little product thankfully, but I'd like Dave to give me hand taking down the booth," Sheridan said. "Though I suspect he's dreaming about helping you."

"You can break it down yourself," Eve said. "Dave has important work yet to do. I don't mean that you're not important, Nova, but he has other work to do."

"Hello, everyone," Rajiv said. "I hope you've all had a successful expo."

"We have," Eve said. "Although I doubt the departed see it that way."

"Very true. I will be holding them close as I go forward."

Eve nodded. "We all will."

One and Two were next to join us.

"Gentlemen," Sheridan said, his attention on One, "you had a narrow escape on the stage. You all right?"

"It was terrifying, but we're used to that kind of thing."

"And to be truthful," Two said, "it brought a flurry of last-minute business. They should have kept the expo open till midnight. We've been busier than ever."

"You ought to grab a hold of some believers to provide testimonials," Sheridan said, "bring them along to the next expo."

"Thank you for the suggestion," One said. "Dr. Unger gave us a wonderful testimonial. We could ask him to speak."

"Dave? I wouldn't have pegged you for that. Care to give us a preview before everyone gets here?"

"You'd have to ask Nova. How's our sex life so far? Everything pretty extraterrestrial for you?"

"I'm not touching that," she said.

"How is everybody doing?" Madame Vadama asked.

"We were talking about sex," Rajiv said.

"There are some things one can rely on."

That's when Lucky walked by the booth and touched his chin.

At the adult fantasy baseball camp I'd been to in Vero Beach, the coaches had taught us about signs; touching your chin meant something else was coming. Was Lucky just letting me know he was there, or saying *Watch out—the forces are coming to the plate*?

"I'm here," Dennis said. "What a bountiful day this has been. It's too bad we're not open all week."

"We're with you on that," Sheridan said. "Host another one soon."

"You can rest assured I will. Already reaching out to venues. So what's this all about? We going to open a bottle of champagne? That's what I'll be doing on the stage in a minute."

"We're waiting for Candy and Phillippe."

Eve said she'd round them up but no sooner had she said it than they entered the booth.

"Sorry to keep everyone waiting. It's been a madhouse. We have an event to go to. I hope this won't take long."

It seemed like I was on the clock.

CHAPTER EIGHTY-TWO

Another Way

IT WAS THE scene out of *Animal Crackers* with Groucho Marx singing "Hello, I Must be Going." As if pulling off a reveal wasn't hard enough, now people wanted to leave after they'd barely arrived. I'm a classroom teacher so I'm used to that, and the power of a grade is usually enough to keep my students in their seats. Here and now, I had nothing at my disposal but partial truths. So that's what I ran with.

"Thank you all for coming. I don't want this to take long, and when we're done we'll have found the person or persons responsible for the deaths of our neighbors. So without further ado, the first person to leave will be the killer trying to make their escape."

I quickly made eye contact with everyone. No one moved.

Sometimes I sacrifice truth for dramatic effect.

"I believe I know who committed the murders. I need your efforts to confirm the matter. As is often the case in life, each of us holds a piece of the puzzle, which means collectively we can reveal whodunit. We have an array of talent and skills between us, and we're going to put them to use.

"Take a moment. Think. Why have these murders occurred?

While they could be random, I don't think any of us believe that. Rather, someone has a reason and a methodology."

I gestured toward One and Two. "Our explorers believe their touch is lethal. If that's true, there's no direct motive, just misfortune in play. So let's hold off on that for now and consider who else might be responsible, and why and how they killed."

"We can do that," One said, "but it's a waste of time. We're the guilty party. If it would help, we can touch you right now and prove it."

How far was I willing to go for my work? I'm not the first person to ask that question, but it could be my last.

"If we're to pursue that line of inquiry, it would be preferable to drive over to a UCLA research lab and test your lethality on a rat."

"We've done that," Two said. "Well, not the UCLA part. We can't kill animals. Only people."

"Well, that's somewhat comforting. But I'll wait a bit on the touching."

"For someone so sure, you seem awfully hesitant," Phillippe said.

"I'll not deny it," I said. "But let's see if we can uncover other means that we can have greater confidence in. There are those among us who are knowledgeable about toxins. Anyone want to take a guess at what might be at play here?"

"Some plants are poisonous," Eve said.

No one expanded on that, and since the killer wouldn't volunteer ibogaine, I'd have to coax it out.

"Those of you who've read my books might be familiar with one particular substance."

"In the ones I've read," said Nova, "everyone gets shot."

"That's true too, yet in the Music book there was a different way."

"That Hunter Thompson drug," Eve said.

"Acid?" Rajiv said. "You're saying they OD'd on acid?"

"No, not exactly. While Hunter ingested a pharmacopeia of

drugs, this wasn't one of them. He just wrote about a presidential candidate taking it, though I think it was a joke."

"Oh, yeah," Sheridan said. "You mean the drug that restricts your mobility."

"Right. Ibogaine. Which if taken in large doses can paralyze you. Someone could have gotten our victims to drink it, and then shot them up with a lethal dose of something after they were paralyzed."

"You mean like aconite?" Eve said. "It's the queen of poisons. It kills you instantly if you drink it. But that's the root. I use the aconite flower in my balms."

"Not many poisonous plants kill instantly, but a cocktail of ibogaine and aconite could have done the trick. The pathologists will soon determine if that was the case."

"Why would someone have drunk such a thing?" Candy asked.

"I gotta tell you," One said, "some of the potions I've sampled here are not very tasty."

"I agree. I tried that Noni fruit drink," Madame Vadama said. "It smelled and tasted like vomit."

"Yeah, I had to throw out the drink I got," I said. "But if you were told it was a magic elixir you might hold your nose and swallow it."

"We do have to go soon," Candy said. "But so what if the killer had them take ibogaine or Noni or anything else? How they got killed is not as important as who did it and why."

"That's true," I said. "But what if the killer chose the method because they'd read my book and wanted to show me up?"

"I've never read any of your books," Two said. "They're not that popular. And why would someone choose that method anyway?"

"That's what I want you to answer."

CHAPTER EIGHTY-THREE

Revealing

TIME WAS MARCHING on and they were getting antsy. As much as I enjoy talking, I know that others would rather talk than listen to me. If I wanted to keep their focus I'd need to get them more involved.

"What do our chiropractor and two tantric practitioners have in common? Do you see a link between them?"

"Aside from being across the aisle from each other?" One asked.

"All our booths are close by," Eve said. "The exception is Dennis, who doesn't have a booth."

"How come he's here?" Rajiv asked.

"Yes, how come I'm here?"

"Eve, can you answer that?"

"Certainly. It's your aura."

"What about my aura?"

"It's dark. All of our auras are dark. You're connected to us."

"I don't think so. My aura looks fine to me."

"Perhaps you're misreading it," Madame Vadama said.

"Impossible." He dismissed us with the wave of an arm. "I have to go. I'm expected on the stage."

"I hear you. We all want to be someplace else doing something else. But hold on though. We have nearly all the pieces of the puzzle," I lied. "What other things in common do the deceased have?"

"Services to offer?" Nova said.

"Bingo. We're providers. We provide something that's supposed to make life better. Sometimes our help has helped others; sometimes it's hindered."

"Did the murderer use one of our services and get hurt by it?" asked Candy.

"Let me ask you. How might a person who'd come to you for tantric sex get hurt?"

"Hard to say. We primarily just advise people to slow down and focus. How could that hurt?"

"It could hurt you, Dave," Sheridan said. "You're not one for slowing down."

"That's very true. When Candy and I did exercises together it was difficult for me to attend to the moment."

"You think that someone got so upset about not being able to stay in the moment that they killed Gordon and Saffron?" Nova said. "That's far-fetched."

"Yes, it is." I turned to Rajiv. "You've been to one of the tantric-sex parties. Did anything happen there that might have been upsetting?"

"Just the usual. Some men ejaculate too soon. Others can't get it up. And no one has a perfect body so maybe they were shamed."

Everyone gave each other the once over. No one's clothed body looked shame-worthy to me, but shame is often something you bequeath upon yourself.

"Let me ask you, Candy and Phillippe, is there anything that might have caused a person to be upset with you?"

"People have been upset because we didn't allow them in. And we had to kick out a few who misbehaved."

"Misbehaved?" Two said.

"People can sometimes get drunk or abusive or refuse to respect another's boundaries."

"And you'd remember someone who'd behaved like that if they were here?" I asked.

"Of course," Candy said, "but Phillippe and I haven't been at all of our events. Saffron and Gordon did tell us about having to expel some people, but we've all had difficult situations to handle."

If someone present had been kicked out of a soirée, they weren't showing it, but it did explain why the two practitioners might have been killed.

"What about Dr. Ketchall? What could he have done that would be so upsetting to someone?"

"Any number of things," Rajiv said. "He could have caused permanent damage. Like all of us, when he first opened his practice he surely made mistakes."

"If that's true," One said, "why not kill him then?"

"Unless the mistake was recent," Nova said. "Or the injury he caused became steadily worse. And as it inflamed, so did they."

"Dave, we have possible motives and means," Sheridan said. "What we don't have is someone to blame."

CHAPTER EIGHTY-FOUR
Someone to Blame

SHERIDAN WAS RIGHT. We didn't have someone to blame. Time to up the ante.

"You all have specialist skills, interests, talents, and abilities. You've tapped into sources that have enriched your lives and the lives of those who are fortunate to have crossed your paths. The time has come for you to use your unique skills to name the killer. Let's start with Madame Vadama. Can you use your psychic powers to see into the truth?"

"I could have us all draw cards, but I can't guarantee the answer will be clear."

"Let me help you," I said. "The other day, I suggested something that might help you. Do you recall what that is?"

"You told me several things."

"Yes, we've had several positive future-focused conversations regarding the similarities in our professions."

"Ah, yes, the more I conjure it, the clearer it becomes. I do see us being able to uncover the killer. I see them surrendering to us, yet not without resistance."

"If you continued to conjure on it, might you be able to identify the killer?"

"The veil is lifting. Like a golden goose taking off."

"That's what I was thinking. Say no more now. What about you, Rajiv? Examine all of us. Is there someone whose chakras are out of balance?"

"I—"

"Wait. Let me stop you there. I'll come back to you. I know you can and want to disclose the culprit, but first let's give others a chance."

I suspected Rajiv was grateful for the reprieve; he probably knew as much as I knew about how the killer's chakra's were tuned. Not least because he'd been distracted by the group of onlookers who'd gathered by the edge of the booth.

Bennett was having a hard time containing himself, Louise was attired in such a way that it was impossible not to gawk at her, and Lucky's eye appeared to be roving all over Candy. Meanwhile, Rip's eye was roving all over Louise and Bennett. Further down the aisle were Mr. and Mrs. Russo, Caddy, and Harry the security guard.

"Eve, you read auras. When you look at us, is there anyone who stands out?"

"Yes—"

"I'm sorry to interrupt, but don't point a finger yet. Hold your thoughts for a minute.

"How about you, Sheridan? Can you spot anyone whose past lives may be catching up to them? Wait, hold off on sharing that for now, as I know how you're going to answer that.

"Candy and Phillippe, you're more knowledgeable than most about how we all interact with our bodies. Is there someone among us whose bearing indicates they're not at peace with themselves? Perhaps they got hurt at one of your parties and then went to Dr. Ketchall for help. Maybe they blame the three victims for the hurt they've suffered."

I paused for a nanosecond.

"I can tell you know, and I want to ask you to keep it to yourself an exotic drug. I killed them with arsenic, just like Agatha Christie. You really need to check your ego at the door."

I heard the shot but didn't feel the bullet.

Dennis slumped.

Rip lowered his pistol.

And Bennett jumped up and down, yelling, "I got him! I got him!"

CHAPTER EIGHTY-SEVEN
Number Ten

BEDLAM ENSUED. SOME ran, others screamed, the security guard came over, and even though Dennis had said it wasn't all about me I still felt pretty full of myself.

I hadn't wanted him to die—public disgrace and humiliation for him and a modicum of applause and recognition for me would have been sufficient—but better him than me.

Shame is a nasty emotion. It festers and chafes your insides and fans the flames of anger. Usually, it fades with time. But not always.

Dennis knew the killings would draw crowds and the profit motive had tipped his decision scale. Killing two birds with one stone might have been too much to resist. It wasn't rational, but killing rarely is. I understood his heart but that didn't justify his actions. And while I don't believe in an eye for eye, he'd taken others' lives and paid in kind.

Rip came up to me.

I thanked him for saving my life and hugged him. "That was too close for comfort."

"I had you covered all the way. I didn't want to kill him, but I couldn't let him kill you. Not after last night."

"I'm certainly glad to hear that."

"Wow. That's so wrong. Like my Aunt Shovesta who thought she was gaining weight only to one day drop a kid out of the shoot. In all probability, he read your name tag."

"I never saw him glance at it. I'd have known, wouldn't I? Although I did sort of miss the fact that Madame Vadama had read my name tag."

"You didn't like him either," Lucky said.

"True, and maybe that clouded my thinking. But I knew having everyone point the finger would trigger the killer. They'd be outed, and that would prompt them to seize the moment. He'd already experienced the awfulness of being pointed at and taunted. He'd have wanted to try to control that situation. Killers have their own big egos. They want to be at the top of the heap, even if it's a criminal one."

"That's caca too. Everyone else pointed at the wrong person."

"It's the woo-woo, Lucky. It gets you in unfamiliar and unexplainable ways. If he'd waited for everyone to point he could have walked away, but he didn't take that chance. If he'd waited and he'd been pointed at, the story would have been about everyone's woo-woo skills. By speaking up first he made it about him. Because despite being a doubter, at a deeper level he wanted to believe. We all want to believe in something greater than us, and when it came down to it, he didn't want to bet against it."

"Doc, he made a bad bet. You know who made a good one? Bennett. He hired me to become his director of security now that he's about to be a big-time movie guy. So I'm moving out here for a while and seeing how things go."

"That ought to be fun."

That left one person in my congratulatory queue.

Nova. I'd seen her waiting for me and liked that she was. I took a little of number ten and rubbed it on my palm.

She hugged me, which I took as a positive sign.

"I'm glad he didn't kill you."

"Me too. Very glad."

"I've been considering…"

"Intentions?"

"Yeah. And I'm not going to change my intentions, my timeline, my goals, or much of anything."

"Sounds like there might be an exception there."

"Yeah. There is. You. You're the exception. We'll have to wait and see how things play out, but, for now, take me someplace other than Zucky's."

The End

This is a book of fiction, which means there's more truth here than I care to admit. There was no Whole Life Expo at the Santa Monica Civic in 1985, but there were many woo-woo conventions/conferences/gatherings, and I've tried to do a fair job of representing the various practices of the metaphysical and alternative healing arts. Still, I've taken a few liberties.

Zucky's was a long-standing deli that's no longer standing. I often went there in high school and once said something funny that made my friend spit a pickle out through his nose. That was the highlight of my comedic life.

If you'd like a peek into what the future holds for David, take a look at what comes after the Acknowledgments.

ACKNOWLEDGMENTS

I need to honor and give out some positive vibrations to the practitioners of the woo-woo arts. I'm sure there are other names they'd like to be called, but the title came to me one night and it stuck. I don't know exactly what woo-woo means but to me it's all those not easily explainable things that happen. I certainly believe that many people have tapped into the resources within and outside of themselves in ways that others of us have yet to do. I know we're capable of way more than we know, and some day in the future some of what we call woo-woo will be common practice and some of it won't.

One piece of woo-woo that I don't doubt is this: when I start my books I have little more than a title. From there a book evolves. Call it the creative process, woo-woo or whatever. It's been good to me.

My family and friends will find themselves and their characteristics sprinkled throughout the book. I thank them for their inspiration and the special woo-woo I find with them.

My editor, Louise Swainston, told me I was a storyteller. I never thought of myself that way. Her telling me that has helped me drift off course less often and focus more on the story. Cally Worden puts the finishing touches on that story and Beth Hamer makes it all come together. And the artists at Damonza create the cover art and formatting. Add the talents of Jake Robertson, who brings the books to audio life, and you have my writing posse. Thanks to all.

I also need to acknowledge my dog Lefty, who was sick while I wrote much of this book, and whose love and care throughout her healing process brought us ever closer together. I suspect you'll see bits of her in the next book, *A Lesson in Dogs and Murder*.

A LESSON IN DOGS AND MURDER

BEVERLY HILLS KENNEL CLUB DOG SHOW

BEST IN SHOW

DAVID UNGER, PHD

PROLOGUE

"So what's the question again?"

"What's the best dog moment you've ever had? I know you love our dog, but come on, share a scene from your highlight reel."

"I don't think about Pierre that way. I just have this warm feeling when I think of him. We share so many soulful moments it's hard to pick one that stands out."

"That's why we love him. He's happy when we show up, and when we take the time to play with him he loves us all the more. Even if we ignore him, he carries on and doesn't give us any grief."

"Unless we abuse him, which is kinda what's happening here."

"No way."

"Yes way."

"No way."

"Yes way."

Pubescent boys.

"Some of the people here are not good to their dogs. They don't play with them like we do. They yell at them and scold them. They're just like Donny Devlin's parents."

"No way. They're crazy. No one here treats their dog that badly."

"Maybe not, but do you really believe dogs prancing around and having a beauty pageant is a good thing? It's twisted."

"I don't see it that way. These dogs love their owners and are happy to prance around and show off."

"Yeah, they do that. But is that what they really want to do, or what they're trained to do like circus animals?"

I gotta tell you, I wasn't expecting things to start off that way. Well, maybe the "best of" thing wasn't a surprise, but the circus-animal-abuse angle? Not so much. Yet here I was eavesdropping on these two emerging adolescents in the registration line at the Beverly Hills Kennel Club Dog Show.

"They're like service dogs, our best friends."

"We're all service dogs. And unfortunately, dude, we're best friends."

"So come on, my best/worst friend and brother, what's your best dog moment? Let's hear it."

"I don't have one, and don't want to think about it that way. But here's the one that popped up. Our parents were having one of their pool parties, and people were swimming, drinking, and eating. Someone put down their plate and left it. I saw Pierre watching as the person ambled away. Then he trotted over to the plate, finished the barbequed burger, and turned away. He looked right at me. We stared at each other, and he knew he was totally busted and not supposed to do that. But he knew I wouldn't rat him out, so we kinda had a special bonding moment right there."

"That's cool. I can dig naughty. And shared naughtiness is the best. We've had some of that."

They guffawed and high-fived.

"Let's have more this weekend," his brother said.

CHAPTER ONE
I Gotta Come Clean

LET ME PUT my cards on the table. Recently, I met a psychic tarot-card reader, Madame Vadama, who told me she laid out the cards daily and intuited what they meant. I figure that if I'm honest with you and lay out my cards from the get-go, you'll believe what I'm going to tell you. And believe me, it will take trust and goodwill to get us through this story.

Left to my own devices, I wouldn't go to the Beverly Hills Kennel Club Dog Show, an American Kennel Club-sanctioned event that would be awarding championship points—something I knew next to nothing about, but which held importance to those for whom it held importance.

I've had a dog most of my life and have never had a bad encounter with one, although there were two Dobermans behind a fence once that made threatening moves as I snuck by. I like dogs. I like to take walks with mine, roll on the floor, play tug-of-war, and have her roll over so I can rub her stomach. I snuggle up, pet her, talk with her, and occasionally we catch each other being naughty and have our own bonding moment. Spending a weekend watching dogs being groomed, paraded around, and fussed over isn't my preferred way to pass the time. I'd rather watch them running at the beach or chasing one another in a meadow.

But I work for a living. I'm a licensed therapist and work in and out of the box. I see clients in my office, and I see them out in the world where they need me. I'd met Madame Vadama at a woo-woo expo where the terms of my payment were such that I now needed to make up for lost revenue.

And, truthfully, I now make more out of the office than I do in it.

When someone hires me, the clock is running. They usually inform me of which event they want me to attend with them, and depending on the time and location, we agree to a price. I went to the woo-woo expo because I'd agreed to help out a couple of people I'd met at a music festival, and we'd allowed the terms of payment to be fuzzy. Something I learned I didn't want to do again.

I'd also learned a few things about woo-woo, had become significantly smitten with someone, and had been paid with a bottle of Love Potion No. 10, which we'll discuss later.

I've gained a degree of notoriety because of the books I've written and had decided to jump on the American bandwagon and raise my rates. In America, we believe that the more something costs the better it must be. Sure, people value a deal, and they don't always desire or need the best. But, given the choice, most people would assume that the $150-an-hour therapist is better than the $100 one, who is better than the $50 one. That may not be true, but it's what we believe. And if you believe, it's true—it's true for you.

It's fair to say I'm in this for the money. If I'm still being truthful, I'm into a lot of my work for the money. If I weren't getting paid, I wouldn't be doing what I'm doing. I don't like admitting the bottom line, but here it is—I'm not following my heart. It's true. There are other things I'd prefer to do or be than a therapist and teacher of graduate psychology students. Don't get me wrong,

I enjoy what I do. Learn from it. Make a good living from it. But if I weren't getting paid I'd do something else.

That something else I'd be doing is writing, and I'm doing more of that these days. But it doesn't pay all the bills so I can't yet let go of my day job. But enough about my mid-life crisis. As a friend often reminds me, I need to get to the murders faster.

They did happen, but before they took place I got a call from someone who wanted to meet with me regarding something of mutual interest.

Mr. Stevens, whose name has been changed to protect his privacy—as have the names of the rest of the people mentioned— was in his fifties, looked like he belonged to a country club, and was wearing a dark suit that was more tailored than anything I've ever worn.

"If half the stuff you write about in your books is true, you're the perfect person for this job."

"I may embellish things a bit, but I do try to keep the truth in mind. What exactly have you got in mind?"

"I represent someone who would like to hire you."

"Very well. Although clients don't usually send representatives. How come you're here and not them?"

"That's a reasonable question. They'd like to retain their anonymity."

"I can understand that, but I assure you that my clients' confidentiality is not something that only I value—my licensing board would also not be happy if I or anyone compromised some-one's privacy."

"All the same, we will not place you in a position where you need to worry about that."

Which of course got me worrying. I didn't know who they were or what they wanted, which is exactly why I was now worrying.

"I'll need to think it over. I've never done therapy by proxy, although I have read about it and suggested it, so it could work."

"Isn't that unethical?" he said with a slight smirk. "Recommending something you haven't tried and valued?"

"You could see it that way," I said with a phony smile. "I did read about a wife whose husband wouldn't go to therapy, so she went and presented his issues as her own and got help on how to deal with them. Then she implemented what she'd learned with her husband. It seemed to work for them. Not sure if it'll work for us. What exactly are we talking about here?"

I didn't take kindly to his pointing out my unethical behavior. My behavior is borderline at best, and some would say—and I might be among them—that I've stepped over those borders on occasion. With good intentions, I would add. Unfortunately, we don't judge others so much on their intentions as we do on their behavior.

"The interested party would like to hire you to attend the Beverly Hills Kennel Club Dog Show."

"They're going to pay me to attend? The event may not be that popular, but surely they don't have to pay people to attend. Except me. I'd need to be paid."

"Money isn't an issue."

"What is the issue?"

"There are concerns that matters may come to pass such that your particular skills would be welcome."

"So my job description is to go to the show and, if matters come to pass, apply those particular skills to them?"

"Precisely."

"Will you be there? Do I have a connection there? A purpose other than to do my thing?"

"You do."

"Care to elucidate?"

I throw out the fancy words for the fancy clients.

"When I hand you this check and you accept it, I will legally become your client, and what I tell you will remain confidential unless I give you written permission to release something."

He reached into the inside pocket of his expensive suit jacket, took out a blank envelope, and handed it to me. I hesitated. The woo-woo expo had left me with a bottle of Love Potion No. 10, the lovesick blues, and no money.

Inside was a check for one thousand dollars, signed by Mr. Stevens on behalf of Consolidated Industries. That put a stop to any further hesitation.

"I expect that will be sufficient for our session today."

It wasn't that long ago that I'd bumped up my hourly rate to a hundred dollars. To get a thousand for a session was an excellent day's work. And yet I wasn't sure that I was comfortable taking him on as a client. It wasn't so much attending the dog show that troubled me as the "matters may come to pass."

I set my worries aside and we agreed on my fee and expenses. At least I was earning Beverly Hills prices.

Recently I've been working more as the whodunit guy than the how-you-feeling one. I use those how-you-feeling skills to find out whodunit, so it's kind of a package deal. Truthfully, being hired to deal with matters that came to pass could be the kind of work I'd prefer to do more often, although those matters might involve a spike in my blood pressure and even loss of life.

I'd be more confident if I were a better detective, but I seem to be a better revealer. I've learned how to get the suspects together and create some voodoo-therapy magic to expose the guilty party. I'd help myself out if I invested energy into improving my sleuthing skills, but I'm not the studious type.

It was too late for that anyway. I'd need to rely on my instincts again. I'd go with the flow and wait for whatever matters might come to pass.